**"It's not going**  **her, not ready** **g to hurt her. "** **for you."**

She shook her head, and in a season filled with hope, he felt his dwindling once again. No matter how many times it happened, he never got used to it. It never got easier.

"I'm the one who needs to apologize," she told him, turning so that she was looking him in the eye. "I just need to try harder, Flint."

Heartache wasn't something that could be brushed off.

"You're doing great, sweetie. I just..." What? He just what? He'd just called her sweetie. Like they were a couple.

She was looking at him, all wide-eyed and filled with emotion. So close. He leaned. She did, too. And their lips touched.

Maybe he'd meant it to be a light touch. A sweet goodbye to go with the endearment.

Maybe he hadn't been thinking at all.

What Flint knew was that he couldn't let go. Her lips on his... His world changed again and he couldn't let go of them. He moved his lips over hers. Exploring. Discovering. Exploding...

**THE DAYCARE CHRONICLES:**
**Bouncing babies and open hearts**

Dear Reader,

Sometimes we can plan and do and create what we want out of life, and then, in an instant, completely outside our control, things change. We knew who we were, and who we expected to be. And then...we're somebody completely different. To me, the true test of ourselves is who we become after such a change. How much of who we thought we were stays with us?

Flint had his entire future mapped out. He'd not only survived but thrived through a difficult childhood. He'd become a member of the elite, wealthy, respected. And then his past pulls him back in the form of a brand-new baby sister who's been orphaned by his convict mother. So is Flint the respectable guy he's designed himself to be? Or just someone who had to get out of the world in which he'd grown up?

And Tamara—bless her heart—tried and tried to have the life she'd designed for herself. Being a mother had been something she'd taken for granted. Her body just wouldn't go along with the plan and so... she became someone else. She made a great life for herself on purpose, with purpose. And then Flint's baby sister threatened to crumble her.

I hope you'll continue reading, that you'll not only thoroughly enjoy the romance, but that you'll find an extra dab of hope to carry with you into your days.

I love to connect with my readers.
Please find me at www.tarataylorquinn.com,
www.Facebook.com/tarataylorquinnauthor,
on Twitter, @tarataylorquinn,
or join my open friendship board at
www.Pinterest.com/tarataylorquinn/friendship.

All the best,

*Tara*

# An Unexpected Christmas Baby

## Tara Taylor Quinn

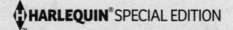

Recycling programs
for this product may
not exist in your area.

ISBN-13: 978-1-335-46611-2

An Unexpected Christmas Baby

Copyright © 2018 by TTQ Books LLC

**Printed in U.S.A.**

www.Harlequin.com

Having written over eighty-five novels, **Tara Taylor Quinn** is a *USA TODAY* bestselling author with more than seven million copies sold. She is known for delivering intense, emotional fiction. Tara is a past president of Romance Writers of America. She has won a Readers' Choice Award and is a seven-time finalist for an RWA RITA® Award. She has also appeared on TV across the country, including *CBS Sunday Morning*. She supports the National Domestic Violence Hotline. If you or someone you know might be a victim of domestic violence in the United States, please contact 1-800-799-7233.

### Books by Tara Taylor Quinn

### Harlequin Special Edition

### *The Daycare Chronicles*

*Her Lost and Found Baby*

### Harlequin Superromance

### *Where Secrets are Safe*

*Her Secret Life*
*The Fireman's Son*
*For Joy's Sake*
*A Family for Christmas*
*Falling for the Brother*

### Harlequin Heartwarming

### *Family Secrets*

*For Love or Money*
*Her Soldier's Baby*
*The Cowboy's Twins*

Visit the Author Profile page
at Harlequin.com for more titles.

For my mom, Penny Gumser, who is
still showing me the meaning of the word *mother*.
And who still reads every word I publish. I love you!

## Chapter One

"Dearly Beloved, we are gathered here today—"

The ceremony had been a dumb idea.

"—Alana Gold Collins to rest. The Father tells us—"

Hands together at his belt buckle, Flint Collins stared down past the crease in his black pants to the tips of his shiny black shoes. *Alana Gold.* Such a lofty name. Like a movie star or something.

*Alana Gold.* Not much about his mother's life had been golden. Except her hair, he supposed. Back when she'd been young and pretty. Before the hard life, the drugs and prison had had their way with her.

"—all will be changed at the last sounding of the bell..."

The Father might have imparted that message. The Bible surely did, according to the preacher he'd hired to give his mother a funeral. *Dearly Beloved*, he'd said. That would be Flint. The dearly beloved. All one of him.

He'd never known any other family. Didn't even know who his father was.

Footsteps sounded behind him and he stiffened. He'd asked her to come—the caseworker he'd only met two days before. To do the...exchange.

*Dearly Beloved.* In her own way Alana had loved Flint deeply. Just as, he was absolutely certain, she'd loved the "inheritance" she'd left him. One he hadn't known about. One he hadn't yet seen. One that had arrived behind him.

"So take comfort..." That was the preacher again. For the life of him, Flint drew a blank on his name as he glanced up and met the older man's compassionate gaze.

He almost burst out with a humorless chuckle. *Comfort?* Was the man serious? Flint's whole life had imploded in the space of a week. Would never, ever, be the same or be what he'd planned it to be. Comfort was a pipe dream at best.

As the footsteps in the grass behind him slowed, as he felt the warmth of a body close to him, Flint stood still. Respectful.

He'd lost his business before it had even opened. He'd lost the woman he'd expected to marry, to grow old beside.

Alana Gold had lost her life.

And in her death had taken part of his.

The preacher spoke about angels of mercy. The woman half a step behind him rocked slightly, not announcing herself in any way other than her quiet presence. Flint fought to contain his grief. And his anger.

His entire life he'd had to work longer, fight harder. At first to avoid getting beaten up. And then to make a place for himself in the various families with whom he'd been temporarily settled. He'd had a paper route at twelve and delivered weekly grocery ads to neighborhoods for pennies, just to keep food on the table during the times he'd been with Alana.

The preacher spoke of heaven.

Flint remembered when he'd been a junior in high school, studying for finals, and had had to spend the night before his test getting his mother out of jail. She'd been prostituting that time. Those were the charges. She'd claimed differently.

But then, Alana's troubles had always been someone else's fault.

In the beginning they probably had been. She'd once claimed that she'd gotten on the wrong track because she'd been looking for a way to escape an abusive father. That was the one part of her story Flint fully believed. He'd met the guy once. Had opted, when given the chance in court, to never have to see him again. Sometimes it worked in a guy's favor to have a caseworker.

After Alana's prostitution arrest during his finals week, he'd expected to be seeing his caseworker again, to have her come to pick him up and take him back to foster care. Instead his mother had been sitting in the living room when he'd gotten home from school the next day, completely sober, her fingernails bitten to the quick, with a plate of homemade chocolate-chip cookies on her lap, worried sick that she'd made him fail his exam.

Tears had dripped down her face as he'd told her of course not, he'd aced it. Because he'd skipped lunch to cram. She'd apologized. Again and again. She'd always said he was the only good thing about her. That he was going to grow up to be something great, for both of them. She'd waited on him hand and foot for a few weeks. Had stayed sober and made it to work at the hair salon—where she'd qualified for men's basic cuts only—for most of that summer.

Until one of her clients had talked her into going out for a good time…

"Let us pray."

Flint's head was already bowed. The brief ceremony was almost over. The closed casket holding his mother's body would remain on the stand, waiting over the hole in the ground until after Flint was gone and the groundskeeper came to lower her to her final rest.

Moisture pricked the backs of his eyelids. For a second, he started to panic like he had the first day he'd gone out to catch the bus for school—a puny five-year-old in a trailer park filled with older kids—and been shoved to the back of the line by every one of them. He could have turned and run home. No one would have stopped him. Alana hadn't been sober enough to know, or care, whether he'd made it to his first day of school. But he hadn't run. He'd faced that open bus door, climbed those steps that had seemed like mountains to him and walked halfway to the back of the bus before sitting.

He was Alana Gold's precious baby boy and he was going to *be* someone.

"Amen." The preacher laid a Bible on top of the coffin.

Amen to that. He was Alana's son and he was going to be someone all right.

"Mr. Collins?"

The voice, a woman's voice, was close to him.

"Mr. Collins? I've got her things in the car, as you asked."

*Her things.* Things for the inheritance Alana had left him. More scared than he could ever remember being, Flint raised his head and turned it to see the brunette standing behind him, a concerned look on her face. A pink bundle in her arms.

Staring at that bundle, he swallowed the lump in his throat. He wasn't prepared. No way could he pass *this* test. In her death, Alana had finally set him up for failure.

She'd unintentionally done it in the past but had never succeeded. This time, though…

He reminded himself that he had to *be* someone.

Brother? Father? Neither fit. He'd never had either.

A breeze blew across the San Diego cemetery. The cemetery close to where he'd grown up, where he'd once seen his mother score dope. And now he was putting her here permanently. Nothing about this day was right.

"Prison records show that your mother had already chosen a name for her. But as I told you, since she died giving birth, no official name has been given. You're free to name her whatever you'd like…"

Prison records and legal documents showed that his forty-five-year-old mother had appointed him, her thirty-year-old son, as guardian of her unborn child. A child Alana had conceived while serving year eight of her ten-year sentence for cooking and dealing methamphetamine in the trailer Flint had purchased for her.

The child's father was listed as "unknown."

He and the inherited baby had that in common. And the fact that their mother had stayed clean the entire time she'd carried them. Birthing them without addiction.

"What did she call her?" he asked, unable to lift his gaze from the pink bundle or to peer further, to seek out the little human inside it.

He'd been bequeathed a little human.

After thirty years of having his mother as his only family, he had a sister.

"Diamond Rose," the caseworker said.

Flint didn't hear any derogatory tone in the voice.

Alana had been gold. A softer metal. He was Flint, a hard rock. And this new member of the family was diamond. Strong enough to cut glass. Valuable and cherished. And Rose… Expensive, beautiful, sweet.

He got Alana's message, even if the world wouldn't. "Then Diamond Rose it is," he said, turning more fully to face the caseworker.

The woman was on the job, had other duties to tend to. She'd already done a preliminary background check but, as family, he had a right to the child even if the woman didn't want to give her to him. Unless the caseworker had found some reason that suggested the baby might be unsafe with him.

Like the fact that he knew nothing whatsoever about infants? Had never changed a diaper in his life? At least not on a real baby. He'd put about thirty of them on a doll he'd purchased the day before—immediately after watching a load of new parenting videos.

He reached for the bundle. Diamond Rose. She'd weighed six pounds, one ounce at birth, he'd been told. He'd put a pound of butter on a five-pound bag of flour the night before, wrapped it in one of the new blankets he'd purchased and walked around the house with it while going about his routine. Figured he could do pretty much anything he might want or need to do while holding it.

Or wearing it. The body-pack sling thing had been a real find. Not that different from the backpacks he'd used all through school, although this one was meant to be worn in front. Put the baby in that, he'd be hands free.

The caseworker, Ms. Bailey, rather than handing him Diamond Rose, took a step back. "Do you have the car seat?"

"I have two," he told her. "In case she has a babysitter and there's an emergency and she needs to be transported when I'm not there." He also had a crib set up in a room that used to be designated as a spare bedroom. Stella, his ex-fiancée, had eyed the unfurnished room as her temporary office until they purchased a home more in line with her wants and needs.

In an even more upscale neighborhood, in other words.

Ms. Bailey held the bundle against her. Flint didn't take offense. Didn't really blame the woman at all. If he were her, he wouldn't want to hand a two-day-old baby over to him, either. But during her two days in the hospital the baby had been fully tested, examined and then released that morning. Released to him. Her family. Via Ms. Bailey. At his request, because he had a funeral to attend. And had wanted Alana's daughter there, too.

"As I said earlier, I strongly recommend a Pack 'n Play. They're less expensive than cribs, double as playpens with a changing table attachment and are easily portable."

Already had that, too. Although he hadn't set it up in his bedroom as the videos he'd watched had recommended. No way was he having a baby sleep with him. Didn't seem... He didn't know what.

He had the monitors. If she woke, he'd have to get up anyway. Walking across the hall only took a few more steps.

"And the bottles and formula?"

"Three scoops of the powder per six ounces of water, slightly warm." He'd done a dozen run-throughs on that. And was opting for boiling all nipples in water just to be safe in his method of cleansing.

He noticed the preacher hovering in the distance. The man of God probably needed to get on to other matters, as well. Flint nodded his thanks and received the older man's nod in return. As he watched him walk away, he couldn't help wondering if Alana Gold would be more than a momentary blip in his memory.

She would be far more than that to her daughter.

Ms. Bailey interrupted his thoughts. "What about child

care? Have you made arrangements for when you go back to work?"

Go back to work? As in, an hour from now? Taking Monday morning off had been difficult enough. With the market closed over the weekend, Mondays were always busy.

And he had some serious backtracking to do at the firm.

In the financial world, things had to be done discreetly and he'd been taking action—confidentially until he knew for sure it was a go—to move out on his own. Somehow his plans had become known and rumors had begun to spread with a bad spin. In the past week there'd been talk that he'd contacted his clients, trying to steal their business away from the firm. A person he trusted had heard something and confided that to him. And then he'd had an oddly formal exchange about the weather with Howard Owens, CEO and, prior to the past week, a man who'd seemed proud to have him around. A man who'd never wasted weather words on Flint. They talked business. All the time. Until the past week.

There was no way he could afford to take time off work now.

"I'm taking her with me." He faced Ms. Bailey, feet apart and firmly grounded. He had to work. Period. "I have a Pack 'n Play already set up in the office."

The woman frowned. "They'll let you have a baby with you at work?"

"My office is private. I'll keep the door closed if it's a problem." The plan was short-term. Eventually he'd have to make other arrangements. He'd only had a weekend to prepare. Had gotten himself trained and the house set up. He figured he'd done a damned impressive job.

Besides, that time Campbell's dog had had surgery, the guy had brought it to the office every day for a week. Kept it in his office. As long as you were a money-maker and didn't get in the way of others making money, you were pretty much untouched at Owens Investments. They were like independent businesses under one roof.

Or so he'd been telling himself repeatedly in the couple of days since he'd realized he couldn't open his own business as planned. Not and have sole responsibility for a newborn. Running a business took a lot more than simply making smart investments. Especially when it was just getting off the ground.

He'd already shut down the entire process. Withdrawn his applications for the licenses required to be an investment adviser to more than five clients and regulated by the SEC in the State of California. Lost his deposit for a proposed suite in a new office building.

If she thought she was going to keep his sister from him now...

Another breeze blew across his face, riffling the edge of the blanket long enough that he caught a flash of skin. A tiny cheek? A forehead?

Panic flared. And then dissipated. That bundle was his sister. His family. Only he could give her that. Only he could tell her about her mother. The good stuff.

Like the times she'd look in on him late at night, thinking he was asleep. Whisper her apologies. And tell him how very, very much she loved him. How much he mattered. How he was the one thing she'd done right. How he was going to make his mark on the world for both of them.

The way she'd throw herself a thousand percent into his school projects, encouraging him, making suggestions, applauding him. How talented she was at crafty things. How she loved to watch sappy movies and made the best popcorn. How she'd want to watch scary movies with him and he'd catch her looking away during the best parts. How she'd never made a big deal out of his mistakes. From spills to a broken window, she'd let him know it was okay. How she'd played cards with him, taught him to cook. How she'd laugh until tears ran down her face. How pretty she used to be when she smiled.

The images flying swiftly through his mind halted abruptly as Ms. Bailey began to close in on him, her arms outstretched.

Hoping to God she didn't notice his sudden trembling, he moved instinctively, settled the weight at the tip of the blanket in the crook of his elbow and took the rest of it on his arm, just as he'd practiced with the flour-and-butter wrap the night before. She was warm. And she squirmed. Shock rippled through him. Ms. Bailey adjusted the blanket, fully exposing the tiniest face he'd ever seen up close. Doll-like nose and chin. Eyelids tightly closed. Puckered little lips. A hint of a frown on a forehead that was smaller than the palm of his hand.

"From what I've seen in pictures, she has your mother's eyes," Ms. Bailey said, a catch in her voice. Because she could hear the tears threatening in his? A grown man who hadn't cried since the first time they'd carted his mother off to prison. He'd been six then.

*She has your mother's eyes.*

He had his mother's eyes. Deep, dark brown. It was fitting that this baby did, too. "We'll be getting on with it, then," he said, holding his inheritance securely against him as he moved toward his SUV, all but dismissing Ms. Bailey from their lives.

Having a caseworker was a part of his legacy that he wasn't going to pass on to his sister.

Reaching the new blue Lincoln Navigator he'd purchased five months before and hadn't visited the prison in even once, he felt a sharp pang of guilt as he realized once again that he'd let almost half a year pass since seeing his mother.

Before he'd met Stella Wainwright—a lawyer in her father's high-powered firm, whose advice he'd come to rely on as he'd made preparations to open his own investment firm—he'd seen Alana at least twice a month. But once he and Stella had hooked up on a personal level, he'd been distracted. Incredibly busy. And...

He'd been loath to lie to Stella about where he'd been—in the event he'd visited the prison—but had been equally unsure about telling her about his convict mother.

As it turned out, his reticence hadn't been off the mark. As soon as he'd told Stella about his mother's death, and the child who'd been bequeathed to him, she'd balked. She'd assumed he'd give the baby up for adoption. And had made it clear that if he didn't, she was moving on. She'd said from the beginning that she didn't want children, at least not for a while, but he'd also seen the extreme distaste in her expression when he'd mentioned where his mother had been when she died, and why he'd never introduced them.

Her reaction hadn't surprised him.

Eight years had passed since he'd been under investigation and nearly lost his career, but the effects were long-lasting. He'd done nothing more than provide his destitute mother with a place to live, but when his name came up as owner of a drug factory, the truth hadn't mattered.

Stella had done a little research and he'd been cooked.

Opening the back passenger door of the vehicle, he gently laid his sleeping bundle in the car seat, unprepared when the bundle slumped forward. Repositioning her, he pulled her slightly forward, allowing her body weight to lean back—and slouch over to the side of the seat.

Who the hell had thought the design of that seat appropriate?

"This might help."

Straightening, he saw the caseworker holding out a brightly covered, U-shaped piece of foam. He took it from her and arranged it at the top of the car seat as instructed. He was pleased with the result. Until he realized he'd placed the sleeping bundle on top of the straps that were supposed to hold the baby in place.

Expecting Ms. Bailey to interrupt, to push him aside to show him how it was done—half hoping she would so she wasn't standing there watching his big fumbling fingers—he set to righting his mistake. The caseworker must be thinking he was incapable of handling the responsibility. However, she didn't butt in and he managed, after a long minute, to get the baby harnessed. He'd practiced that, too. The hooking and unhooking of those straps. Plastic pieces that slid over metal for the shoulder part, metal into metal over the bottom half.

He stood. Waited for a critique of his first task as a... guardian.

Handing him her card, reminding him of legalities he'd have to complete, Ms. Bailey took one last look at the baby and told him to call her if he had any questions or problems.

He took the card, assuring her he'd call if the need arose. Pretty certain he wouldn't. He'd be like any normal...guardian; he'd call the pediatrician. As soon as he had one. Another item he had to add to the list of immediate things to do.

"And for what it's worth..." Ms. Bailey stood there, looking between him and the little sister he was suddenly starting to feel quite proprietary about. "I think she's a very lucky little girl."

Wow. He hadn't seen that coming. Wasn't sure the words were true. But they rang loudly in his ears as the woman walked away.

Standing in the open space of the back passenger door, he glanced down at the sleeping baby, only her face visible to him, and didn't want to shut the door. Didn't want to leave her in the big back seat all alone.

Which was ridiculous.

He had to get to work. And hope to God he could mend whatever damage had been done by his previous plans to leave. He had some ideas there—a way to redeem himself, to rebuild trust. But he had to be at the office to present them.

Closing the door as softly as he could, he hurried to the driver's seat, adjusted the rearview mirror so he could see enough of the baby to know she was there and started the engine. Not ready to go anywhere. To begin this new life.

He glanced in the mirror again. Sitting forward so he could see the child more clearly. Other than the little chest rising and falling with each breath, she hadn't moved.

But was moving him to the point of panic. And tears, too. He wasn't alone anymore.

"Welcome home, Diamond Rose," he whispered.

And put the car in Drive.

## Chapter Two

"Dad, seriously, tell me what's going on." Tamara Owens faced her father, not the least bit intimidated by the massive cherry desk separating him from her. Or the elegantly imposing décor throughout her father's office.

She'd seen him at home, unshaved, walking around their equally elegant five-thousand-square-foot home in boxers and a T-shirt. In a bathrobe, sick with the flu. And, also in a bathrobe, holding her hair while she'd thrown up, sick with the same flu. Her mom, the doctor in the family, had been at the hospital that night.

"You didn't put pressure on me to move home just because you and Mom are getting older and I'm your only child." It was the story they'd given her when they'd bombarded her with their "do what you need to do, but at least think about it" requests. Then her father, in a conversation alone with her, had given Tamara a second choice, an "at least take a month off and stay for a real visit" that had made the final decision for her. She'd gotten the feeling that he needed her home. She'd already been contemplating leaving the East Coast, where she'd fled two years earlier after having lived in San Diego her entire life. Her reputation as an efficiency consultant was solid enough to allow her to branch out independently, rather than work through a firm without fear of going backward. Truth be told, in those two years, she'd missed her folks as much as they'd missed her, in spite of their frequent trips across the country to see each other.

She'd lived by the ocean in Boston, but she missed Southern California. The sunshine and year-round warmth. The two-year lease renting out her place by the beach, not far from the home she'd grown up in, had ended and the time seemed right to make the move back home.

"And you didn't ask me down here to have lunch with you just to catch up, either," she told him. Though his thick hair was mostly gray, her father, at six-two, with football shoulders that had absolutely no slump to them, was a commanding figure. She respected him. But he'd never, ever, made her feel afraid of him.

Or afraid to speak up to him, either.

Her parents, both remarkably successful, independent career people, had raised her to be just as independent.

"I wanted to check in—you know, just the two of us— to see how you're really doing."

Watching him, she tried to decide whether she could take him at face value. There'd been times, during her growing-up years, when she'd asked him for private conversations because her mother's ability to jump too completely into her skin had bothered her. And times when he'd wanted the same. This didn't feel like one of those times. But...

"I'm totally over Steve, if that's what you want to know,"

she told him. "We've been talking for about six months now. Ever since he called to tell me he was getting married. I spoke with him a couple of weeks ago to tell him I was moving home. I care about him as a friend, but there are truly no regrets about our decision to divorce."

The passion between them had died long before the marriage had.

"I was wondering more about the…other areas of your life."

Some of those were permanently broken. She had an "inhospitable" uterus. Nothing anyone could do about that.

"I've come to terms with never having a baby, if that's what you mean." After she'd lost the fourth one, she'd known she couldn't let herself try again. What she'd felt for those babies, even when they'd been little more than blips in an ultrasound, had been the most incredible thing ever. But the devastation when she'd lost them…that had almost killed her. Every single time.

She couldn't do that again.

"There are other ways, Tam."

She shook her head.

"Adoption, for instance."

Another vigorous shake of her head was meant to stop his words.

"Down the road, I mean. When you meet someone, want to have a family…"

She was still shaking her head.

"Just give it some time."

She'd given it two years. Her feelings hadn't changed. Not in the slightest. "Knowing how badly it hurts to lose a child… It's not something I'm going to risk again. Not just because I'm afraid I'd miscarry if I got pregnant again, although it's pretty much assured that I would. But even without that, I can't have children. Whether I lost a child through miscarriage or some other way, just knowing it could happen... I can't take that chance. The last time, I hit a wall. I just don't— I've made my peace with life and I'm happy."

A lot of days she was getting there. Had moments when she *was* there. And felt fully confident she'd be completely there. Soon.

"But you aren't dating."

Leaning forward, she said, "I just got back to town a week ago! Give me time!"

He didn't even blink. "What about Boston? Didn't you meet anyone there?"

"I was hardly ever home long enough to meet anyone," she reminded him. "Traveling all over the country, making a name for myself, took practically every second I had."

The move to Boston had been prompted by an offer she'd had to join a nationally reputed efficiency company. She'd been given the opportunity to build a reputation for herself. To collect an impressive database of statistical proof from more than two dozen assignments that showed she could save a company far more money per year, in many departments, than they'd pay for her one-time services. Her father had seen the results. He'd been keeping his own running tally of her successes.

"You did an incredible job, Tam, I'm not disputing that. I'm impressed. And proud of you, too."

The warmth in those blue eyes comforted her as much now as when she'd been a little kid and fallen off her bike the first time he'd taken off the training wheels. She hadn't even skinned her knee, but she'd been scared and he'd scooped her up, made her look him in the eye and see that she was just fine.

"I guess it's a little hard for me to believe that emotionally you're really doing as well as you say, because I don't see *how* you do it. I can't imagine ever losing you… I don't know how I'd have survived losing four."

"But you *did* lose four, Daddy. You were as excited as anyone when you found out I was pregnant. Heck, you'd already bought Ryan his first fishing rod…"

She still had it, in the back of the shed on her small property. She'd carried Ryan the longest. Almost five months. They'd just found out he was a boy. Everything had looked good. And then…

Through sheer force of will, she stopped the shudder before it rippled through her. Remembering the sharp stabs of debilitating physical pain was nothing compared to the morose emptiness she'd been left with afterward.

"I'm not as strong as you are." Howard Owens's voice sounded…different. She hardly recognized it. Tamara stared at him, truly frightened. Was her father sick? Did her mother know? Was that why they'd needed her home?

Frustrated, she wanted to demand that he tell her what was going on, but knew better. The Owens and their damned independence. Asking for help was like an admission of defeat.

"Of course you are," she told him, ready to hold him up, support him, for whatever length of time it took to get him healthy again. If, indeed, he was sick. She slowed herself down. She'd just been thinking how healthy, robust, strong he looked. His skin as tanned as always, that tiny hint of a belly at his waist… Everything was as it should be. He'd been talking about his golf scores at dinner the night before—until her mother had changed the subject in the charming manner she had that let him know he was going on and on.

Tamara had been warmed by the way her mother had smiled at her father as the words left her mouth—and the way, as usual, he'd smiled back at her.

She and Steve had never had that; they'd never been able to communicate as much or more with a look as they had with words. In the final couple of years, not even words had worked for them…

"Anyway," she continued, pulling her mind out of the abyss, "you're the one who taught me *how* to do it," she said, mimicking him. "It's all about focus, exactly like you taught me. If I wanted to get good grades, I had to focus and study. If I wanted to have a good life, I had to focus on what I wanted. If I wanted to overcome the fear, I had to keep my thoughts on things other than being afraid. And if I want to be a success, I just have to focus on doing the best job I can do. Focus, Dad. That's what you've always taught me and what I've always done. In everything I do."

It was almost like she was telling him how to make it through whatever was bothering him.

He'd always been her greatest example.

Howard's eyes closed for longer than a blink. When he opened them again, he didn't meet her gaze. And for the second time fear struck a cold blow inside her. *Focus on the problem*, she told herself. Not on how she was feeling.

To do that, she had to know the problem.

"What's going on, Dad?" There was no doubt that his call to her asking her to come home had to do with more than missing her. How much more, she had to find out.

"Owens Investments was audited this past spring."

Her relief was so heady she almost saw stars. It was business. Not health. "You've got some misplaced files?" she asked him. "You need me to do a paper trail to satisfy them?" Her Master's in Business Administration had been a formal acknowledgment of her ability, but Tamara's true skills, organization and thoroughness, were what had catapulted her to success in her field. If a paper trail existed, she'd find it. And then know how to better organize the process by which documents were collated so nothing got lost again.

Her father's chin jutted out as he shook his head. "I wish it was missing files. Turns out that someone's been siphoning money from the company for over a year. And I'm not sure it's stopped. If it continues, I could lose everything."

Okay. So, not good news. Also not imminent death. Anything that wasn't death was fixable.

"I need your help, Tam," Howard said, folding his hands on the desk as he faced her. "Money is a vulnerable business. A lucrative one, but vulnerable. If our investors hear there's money missing, they'll get nervous. There could be a massive move out…"

She could see that. Was more or less a novice about the ins and outs of what he did, but she knew how companies worked. And the importance of consumer trust.

"I was hoping I'd be able to figure out what's going on myself, no need to alarm you or bring you home, but I haven't been able to find the leak. I need you to come in and do what you do. To give us a once-over, presumably to see if you can save us money. In reality, I'm hoping that you can give everything more of a thorough study without raising suspicions the way it would if I was taking a deeper look."

She nodded, recognizing how hard it was for her father to have to ask for help. Thinking ahead. Focusing on the job.

"People are going to know I'm your daughter. They might be less comfortable speaking with me."

He shook his head again. "I've thought of that. A few will know, of course. Roger. Emily. And Bill. For the rest, it works in our favor that you kept your married name because it was the name you became known under in the business world. People will have no reason to suspect."

Roger Standish, Emily Porter and Bill Coniff. CFO, VP and Director of Operations, respectively. Her father's very first employees when he'd first started out. She'd met them all but it wasn't as if he'd been close friends with his business associates. He was closer to his clients. Many of those she knew better than her own aunts and uncle. Still, none of his top three people would rat her out to the employees. Unless...

"What if the problem rests with one of those three?"

"I guess we'll find that out," he said, raising a hand and then running it over his face. Clearly he'd been dealing with the problem for a while. Longer than he should have without saying anything. She was thirty-two, not thirteen.

"Does Mom know?"

"Of course. She wanted me to call you home immediately."

"You should have."

"Your happiness and emotional health mean more to me than going bankrupt."

Feeling her skin go cold again, she stared at him. Was it that bad?

"Your well-being is one of the top factors that affects my emotional health," she couldn't help pointing out to him.

With a nod, he conceded that.

He was asking for her help. Nothing else mattered.

"How soon can I start?" she asked.

"That was going to be my question."

"When you finally got around to telling me you needed something..." The slight dig didn't escape him.

"I was going to tell you today. I was just having a bit of trouble getting to it. You've been through so much and I don't like putting more on you..."

"I make my living by having companies put more on

me. It's what I do, what I strive for." She grinned at him. He grinned back.

Her world felt right again.

"So…is now too soon?"

"Now would be great. But…there's one other thing."

The knot was back in her stomach. *Please, not his health.* Had he waited until the stress had taken a physical toll before calling her? "What?"

"I don't want to prejudice or influence your findings, but there's one employee in particular who I think could be the one we're after. Although I wasn't able to find anything concrete that says it's him."

Pulling the tablet she always kept in her bag onto her lap, she turned it on. Opened a new file. "Who is he? And why do you suspect him?"

"His name's Flint Collins. I took him on eight years ago when he was let go by his firm and no one else would hire him. He'd only been in the business a year, but had good instincts. He was up-front about the issues facing him and looked me straight in the eye as we talked. He was… He kind of reminded me of myself. I liked him."

Enough to have been blinded by him? "Have I ever met him? Flint Collins?"

"No." Her father didn't have office parties at home. And rarely ever attended the ones he financed at the office.

"So what were his issues eight years ago?"

Not really an efficiency matter, she knew, unless, of course, he was wasteful to the point of being a detriment to the company. But then, this wasn't just an efficiency case.

This was her father. And she was out for more than saving his firm a few dollars.

"His mother was indicted on multiple drug charges. She'd been running a fairly sophisticated meth lab from her home and was dealing on a large enough scale to get her ten years in prison."

Had to be tough. But… "What did that have to do with him, specifically?"

"The trailer she lived in was in his name. As were all the utilities. Paid by him every month. He had regular contact with his mother. He'd already begun to make decent money and was investing it, so he was worth far more than average for a twenty-two-year-old just out of college. Investigators assumed that part of his wealth came from his cut of his mother's business and named him as a suspect. They froze his assets. Any investors he had at the firm where he worked got scared and moved their accounts. It was a bad deal all the way around."

"Was he ever formally charged?" She figured she knew the answer to that. He wouldn't be working for her father as an investment broker if he had been. But she had to ask.

"No. He says he had no idea what his mother had been doing. Seemed to be in shock about the whole thing, to tell you the truth. A warrant for all his accounts and assets turned up no proof at all that he'd ever taken a dime from anyone for anything. All deposits were easily corroborated with legitimate earnings."

"How'd he do for you?"

"Phenomenal. As well as I thought he might. He's one of our top producers. Until recently, I never suspected him of anything but being one of the best business decisions I'd ever made."

"What happened recently?"

"He hooked up with a fancy lawyer. His spending habits changed. He bought a luxury SUV, started taking exotic vacations, generally living high. I'm not saying he couldn't afford it, just that a guy who's always appeared to be conservative with his own spending was suddenly flashing his wealth."

As in…he'd come into new wealth? Or felt like he'd tapped into a bottomless well? Or was running with a faster crowd and needed more than he was making?

"There's more," her father said. "Last week Bill told me he'd heard from Jane in Accounting that she'd heard from a friend of hers in the office of the Commissioner of Business Oversight that Collins was planning to leave. That he was filing paperwork to open his own firm. Bill says he heard that Collins was planning to take his book of business with him."

She disliked the guy. Thoroughly.

"He can't do that, can he? Solicit his clients away from you?"

"No, but that doesn't mean he won't drop a word in an ear here and there." Howard slowly tapped a finger on the edge of his desk, seeming to concentrate on the movement. "As I said, money is a vulnerable business. His clients trust him. They'll follow him of their own accord."

"So he's going to be direct competition to the man who took a chance on him?" *Hate* was such a strong word. She didn't want it in her vocabulary. Anger, on the other hand…

"I left another firm to start Owens Investments." Her father's words calmed her for the immediate moment. "He was doing what I did. Following in my footsteps, so to speak. I just didn't see it coming from him. I thought he was happy here."

"Unless he's leaving because he knows someone is on to the fact that money is being misplaced."

"That's occurred to me, too. About a hundred times over the past week. A guy who's opening his own business doesn't usually start spending lavishly. And if he was the decent guy I thought he was, he would at least have let me know his plans to leave. Which is what I did when I was branching out.

"And, like I said, he's the only one here who's made any obvious changes in routine or lifestyle over the past year. I did some checking into health-care claims and asked around as much as I could, and no one seems to be going through any medical crisis that would require extra funding. I'm not aware of any rancorous divorces, either."

"So… I start now and my first visit is to Mr. Flint Collins."

Howard nodded. "We need to get a look at every file he has while everything is still here."

Which might take some time. "Do you know how soon he's planning to leave?"

"Technically, I don't actually know that he's going. Like I said, this is all still rumor. He's given me no indication or made any official announcement about his plans."

"But it could be soon?"

Howard shrugged. "Could be any day. I just hope to God it's not. Even if he's not the one who's been stealing from me, he's going to do it indirectly unless I can get to his clients first. I've already started reaching out—making sure everyone's happy, letting them know that if there's any question or discomfort at all, to contact me. I'll take on more accounts myself rather than lose them."

Even then, her dad would have to be careful. He couldn't appear to be stabbing a fellow broker in the back just to keep more profits for himself. She did know *some* things about his business. She also remembered a time when she'd been in high school and another broker had left the firm. Her dad had talked to her mother about a party for the investors who'd be affected, which they'd had and then he'd acted on her advice as to how to deliver his news. She just couldn't remember what that advice had been. What stuck in her mind was that her father had taken it.

Which had given a teenage Tamara respect for, and faith in, both of them.

Standing, she asked her dad for a private space with a locking door that she could use as an office. Told him she'd need passwords and security clearance to access all files. And suggested he send out a memo, or however they normally did such things within the company, to let everyone know, from janitorial on up, that she'd be around and why, giving him wording suggestions. Everything that came with her introductory speech on every new job she took. She had a lot of work to do.

But first she was going to introduce herself to Flint Collins.

While her heart hurt for the young man who, from the sound of things, had a much more difficult upbringing than many—certainly far more difficult than she'd had—that didn't give him the right to screw over her family. Karma didn't work that way.

## Chapter Three

Flint took the back way into his office. Leaving the base of the car seat strapped into the back of his SUV, he unlatched the baby carrier, carefully laid a blanket over the top and hightailed it to his private space.

Lunchtime at Owens Investments meant that almost everyone in Flint's wing would be out wining and dining clients, or holed up in his or her office getting work done. His door was the second from the end by the private entrance—because he'd requested the space when it became available. He wasn't big on socializing at work and hadn't liked being close to the door on the opposite end of the hall, which led to reception.

He'd never expected to be thankful that he could sneak something inside without being seen. That Monday he was.

Everyone was going to know. He just needed time to see Bill. His boss, Bill Coniff, was Director of Operations and, he was pretty sure, the person who'd ratted him out before he was ready to go to Howard Owens with his plan to open his own firm. Jane in Accounting had told him about the rumor going around, and said she'd interrupted Bill telling Howard. According to Jane, Bill had twisted the news to make it sound like Flint had been soliciting his current clients to jump ship with him.

Flint would get out of the business altogether before he'd do that.

Business was business. Howard had taught him that. Flint was good at what he did and could earn a lot more money over the course of his career by having his own firm. Could make choices he wasn't currently permitted to make regarding certain investments because Howard wasn't willing to take the same risks.

He felt that to live up to his full potential, he had to go, but he'd been planning to do it ethically. With Howard fully involved in the process—once there was a solid process in which to involve him.

But in less than a week his life had irrevocably changed. Forever. His focus now had to be on making enough money to support a child, not taking risks. To provide a safe, loving home. And to have time to be in that home with the child as much as possible.

How the hell he was supposed to go about that, he had no real idea. First step had been watching all the videos. Buying out the baby store.

And the next was to humble himself, visit Bill Coniff and ensure his current job security. To beg if it came to that.

He spent a few minutes setting up the monitor system he'd purchased for his office, putting the remote receiver in his pocket and taking one last glance at the baby carrier he'd placed on the work table opposite his desk. The floor was too drafty, the couch too narrow. What if she cried and moved her arms and legs a lot and the carrier fell off?

Ms. Bailey had said that the infant had been fed before she'd brought her to the gravesite. Apparently she ate every two hours and slept most of the rest of the time. By his math, that gave him half an hour to get his situation resolved before she'd need him.

Testing the monitor by talking into it and making sure he heard his own voice coming out of his pocket, he left the room, closing the door behind him. Should he lock it? Somehow, locking a baby in a place alone seemed dangerous. Neglectful. But he couldn't leave the door unlocked. Anyone could walk down that hallway and steal her away.

Was he wrong to vacate the room at all?

People left babies in nurseries at home and even went downstairs. Bill's office was two doors away from his. He'd see anyone who walked by. Unless whoever it was came in through the private door. Only employees had access to that hall.

There were security cameras at either end.

If there was a fire and he was hurt, a locked door would prevent firefighters from getting to Diamond Rose.

Decision made, he left the door unlocked.

"Please, Bill, I'm asking you to support me here. I'm prepared to plead my case to Howard. Just back me up on it. I don't know who started spreading the rumors or how far they've reached, but I'm fairly certain they made it to Howard's office…"

On her way to knock on the door of one Flint Collins, Tamara stopped in her tracks. Standing in a deserted private hallway in two-and-a-half-inch heels and her short black skirt with its matching short jacket, plus the lacy camisole her mother had bought to go with the ensemble, she felt conspicuous. But something told her not to move. She'd dressed for a "professional" lunch with her father, not for real business. But business was at hand.

"You're telling me you didn't file paperwork to open your own investment firm?"

She recognized Bill's voice coming from the office with his name on the door. Based on what her father had told her, she figured Bill had to be speaking with Flint Collins. Did her father know Bill was intending to handle the matter?

"No. I'm not saying that. I'm telling you I no longer have plans to do that and would like to do whatever I need to, to ensure my job security here."

"Your plans to hurt this company by soliciting our customers didn't work out, so now I should trust that you're here to stay?"

Bill was in the process of firing the guy? He couldn't! Not yet! She needed time to investigate him while his files were all still in his office at the company. While he didn't know he was being watched.

"I did not, nor did I intend, to solicit anyone. I intended to have a meeting with Howard and do things the right way."

"And now you don't plan to leave anymore."

"Now, in light of the rumors that went around last week, I'd like to guarantee that I have job security here and I was hoping for your cooperation. You know the money I make for this firm, Bill."

"*You* know how important trust is to this firm."

Tamara took a step forward. She couldn't let Bill fire the man, but wasn't sure how to prevent that from happening without exposing more than she could if she was going to be effective in her task.

"I'm willing to sign a noncompete clause to prove my trustworthiness."

"Wow, I like the sound of that!" Tamara burst into the room with a smile that she hoped Bill would accept at face value. She and her father had decided that even his top people shouldn't be told her true reason for being there. At the moment, they could only trust each other.

But he'd called all three of them before she'd left his office, telling them she was going to be doing an efficiency study and that he'd like their cooperation in keeping her relationship to him quiet. Howard wanted to make sure that as she moved about the company, she'd have their full support. She was working under her married name of Frost. Howard had explained that he'd thought people would be less nervous around her if they didn't know she was his daughter.

"Tamara? So good to see you!" Bill turned to her, an odd combination of welcoming smile and bewildered frown warring on his face.

"As you know, Bill, I'm here to study operations on all levels and find ways for Owens Investments to show a higher profit by running more efficiently," she said, holding out her hand to shake his.

Luckily she had her professional spiel down pat. Normally, though, the words weren't accompanied by a pounding heart. Or the sudden flash of heat that had surfaced as she'd looked from Bill to his conversation mate and met the brown-eyed gaze of the compelling blond man she'd been predisposed to dislike on sight.

At first Flint had absolutely no idea who the beautiful, auburn-haired woman with the gold-rimmed green eyes was as she interrupted the meeting upon which his future security could very well rest.

Bill quickly filled him in as he introduced the efficiency expert Howard Owens had hired. Apparently a memo had been sent to Flint and all Owens employees in the past hour. He, of course, had been busy burying his mother and becoming a guardian/father/brother and hadn't gotten to the morning's email yet.

Thinking of the baby girl he'd left sleeping in his office, he reached for the monitor in his pocket, thumb moving along the side to check that the volume was all the way up. He'd been gone almost five minutes. Didn't feel good about that.

"It seems to me, Bill, that if we have a broker on staff who's willing to sign a noncompete clause, then we should give him that opportunity. If he doesn't produce, we can still let him go. If he does, our bottom line has more security. We don't lose either way. Efficient. I like it."

Flint wasn't sure he liked *her*. But he liked what she was saying, since it meant Diamond Rose would have security.

"Unless you know of some reason we shouldn't keep him on?" she asked. "Other than what I just overheard, that he'd been thinking about opening his own firm?"

She looked at him. He didn't deny the charge. But he wasn't going to elaborate. Other than Bill, Howard Owens was the only one to whom Flint would report.

It seemed odd that this outside expert happened to be in the hall just as he'd been speaking with Bill. As though some kind of fate had put her there.

Or a mother in heaven looking out for her children?

The idea was so fanciful, Flint had a second's very serious concern regarding his state of mind. But another completely real concern cut that one short. His pocket made a tiny coughing sound.

All three adults in the room froze. Staring at each other.

And Flint's brand-new little girl made another, half-crying sound. In a pitch without weight. Or strength.

The woman—Tamara Frost, as Bill had introduced her—stared at his pocket. For a second there she looked… horrified. Or maybe sick.

"Not that it's any of my business but…do you have a newborn baby cry as your ringtone?" Her voice, as she looked up at him, sounded professionally nonjudgmental— although definitely taken aback.

Probably didn't happen often… Guys with the sound of crying babies in their pockets during business meetings.

Diamond Rose released another small outburst. Twenty minutes ahead of schedule. He had to get back to her. His first real duty and he was already letting her down. He'd had no time to prepare the bottle, as he'd expected to.

"I'm sorry," he said, looking from Bill to their expert and then heading to the door. "I have to get this."

Let them think it was his phone. And that the call was more important at that moment than they were.

Just until he had things under control.

## Chapter Four

She was coming down with something. Wouldn't you know it? First day of the most important job of her life to date—because it was for her father, her family—and she was experiencing hot flashes followed by cold shivers.

That could only mean the flu.

Crap.

"So…you're good with keeping him on?" She looked at Bill and then back to the doorway they'd both been staring at. She'd been listening for Mr. Collins's "hello" as he took the call that was important enough for him to leave a meeting during which he'd been begging for his job. She'd wanted to hear his tone of his voice as he addressed such an important caller.

Business or pleasure?

"Your father said you're the boss." Bill's words didn't seem to have any edge to them.

"Well, he's wrong, of course." She was smiling, glad

to know she didn't have to worry about stepping on at least one director's toes. "But it makes sense, from an efficiency standpoint, to keep on a broker who's willing to sign a noncompete clause. Unless you know of some reason he should go? I heard him say he makes the company money. Is that true?"

"He's one of our top producers."

She knew that already, but there was no reason, as an efficiency expert who hadn't yet seen her first file, that she should.

"You have some hesitation about him?"

She'd asked Bill twice if there was a reason Flint Collins shouldn't stay on. Bill hadn't replied.

He gave a half shrug as he looked at her and crossed to his desk, straightening his tie. "None tops the offer he made a few minutes ago. Still, I don't like having guys around that I can't trust."

He had her total focus. "He's given you reason to mistrust him?"

Bill shook his head. "Just the whole 'opening his own shop' thing."

"It's what my dad did—left a firm to start Owens Investments. And you helped him do it."

"We did it the right way," Bill said. "The first person your father told, before taking any action, was his boss. None of this finding out from a friend in the recorder's office. Makes me wonder what else he isn't telling us…"

Made her wonder, too.

"I'm going over all the company files. He'll know that as soon as he reads his email. Seems like if he's untrustworthy, he'll have a problem with that."

"If he's got anything to hide, you aren't going to find it."

Maybe not.

Ostensibly her job was to come up with ways for Owens

to make more money. "He's a top producer and wants to sign a noncompete agreement."

"Right when he was getting ready to go into business for himself," Bill said, frowning. "Like I said, kind of makes you wonder why, doesn't it?"

"Is it possible that any of his applications for the various licenses were turned down for some reason?"

"From what I heard, he'd been fully approved."

"Could you have heard wrong?"

Bill shrugged again. "Anything's possible."

She nodded. She needed to get hold of Flint Collins's files.

"He came to you knowing he had to contend with trust issues and was armed with a plan that benefits Owens Investments," she said. She wasn't sure how to interpret that yet. Had he seen that he could make more siphoning off money from her father than he would on his own?

"He's a smart businessman."

"So, are you okay with keeping him on or will you be letting him go?" She couldn't allow him to think it really mattered to her. Or that she intended to push her weight around, beyond efficiency expertise.

If Bill planned to fire Collins right away, she'd go to her father, have him handle the situation. She hoped it didn't come to that.

"Of course I'm keeping him on," Bill said. "He's making us a boatload of money. But I don't trust him and I'll be watching him closely."

Her father had a good man in his Director of Operations. Smiling, Tamara told him so, thanked him and promised to do all she could to stay out of his way.

Shouldn't be hard. She had a feeling Flint Collins would be taking up most of her time.

Maybe an efficiency expert wouldn't be able to find

whatever he might be hiding, or anything he might be doing to rip off her family, but a daughter out to protect her father would.

By whatever means it took.

Tamara was certain of that.

For a man who liked to plan his life down to the number of squeezes left in his toothpaste tube, Flint figured he was doing pretty well to be at his desk, with his computer on, twenty minutes after leaving Bill Coniff's office.

His "inheritance," the tiny being who was now his responsibility for life, lay fed, dry and fast asleep in the car seat–carrier combination, her head securely cushioned by that last little gift from the caseworker. He'd placed her on the table across the room, but sitting at his desk, he wasn't satisfied. The carrier was turned sideways. He couldn't see her full face to know at a glance that her blanket hadn't somehow interfered with her breathing, say if she happened to move in her sleep.

Clicking to open his client list, he crossed the room and adjusted the carrier, turning it to face his desk. Looked at the baby. Noticed her steady breathing.

She had the tiniest little nose. Probably the cutest thing he'd ever seen.

She was going to be a beauty.

Like their mother…

He planned to keep her under lock and key. Away from anyone who could attempt to hurt her…

Taken aback by the intensity of that thought, telling himself he wasn't really losing his mind, he returned to work. Found the client file he wanted. Opened it.

On Friday, before his world had completely crumbled, he'd made an investment that was meant to be short-term. A weekend news announcement had caused the stock to plummet, but it would rise again, for a few days at least, before it either plummeted long-term or—as he hoped— held steady. He figured he'd have five days max. Preferably three. The risk was greater than Howard would want, but the potential return should be remarkable enough to secure his job, at least for now.

As long as the risk paid off.

Flint clicked on certain files, clicked some more. Looked at numbers. Studied market movement. It occurred to him that he should be nervous. If he'd invested at a loss, it could potentially mean his job. He knew Bill had been about to fire him when fate had sent in the consultant Howard had hired.

He wasn't nervous. Flint took risks with the market. But only when his gut was at peace with them. His financial gift was about the only thing he trusted.

Glancing up, he checked his new responsibility. He could see movement as she breathed. Stared as a fist pushed its way out of the blanket. Who'd have thought hands came that small? Or that people did?

She looked far too insecure on that big table made for powerful business deals between grown men and women.

Market numbers scrolled on his screen. They were still going up. But they could take a second rapid dive; his guess was they would. And soon. They'd already climbed higher than he'd conservatively predicted, but not as high as he'd optimistically hoped.

Pushing back from his desk, he crossed the room again, lifted the carrier gently, loath to risk waking his charge. With his free hand, he pulled a chair back to his desk, positioning it next to his seat, along the wall to his left. Away from the door and any unseen drafts. Satisfied, he settled the carrier there, glanced at his computer screen and pushed the button to sell.

At a price higher than he'd hoped.

Five minutes later, the stock started to drop.

He still had his touch. And a fairly good chance of securing his job. Even Bill couldn't argue with the kind of money he'd just made.

As was her way, Tamara studied before she went into action. She didn't take the time she would later spend going over individual accounts, one by one, account by account, figure by figure. But when she approached Flint Collins's office late Monday afternoon, she not only knew every piece of information in his employee file, but she was familiar with every account he'd handled in the nearly eight years he'd been working for her father.

Aside from the part about suspecting that he was stealing from them, she was impressed. And more convinced than ever that if anyone could succeed in taking money from Howard without his knowing, it could be Collins. The man was clearly brilliant.

He'd been a suspect in the drug production and distribution that had put his mother in prison; he'd also grown up with her criminal history. According to a pretty thorough background check, the only consistent influence in his life had been his mother—in between her various stints in jail.

The first of which had come when he was only six. She'd been sentenced to three months. Tamara had seen a list of his mother's public criminal record in his file. Probably there because of Flint's ties to her latest arrest. She'd also seen that the woman was only fifteen years older than her son. A child raising a child.

Funny how life worked. A young girl who, judging by the facts, had been ill-equipped to have the responsibility of a child and yet she'd had one. While Tamara...

No. She wasn't going backward.

Passing Bill's open door, she waved at the director who was on the phone but waved back. Smiled at her. And her heart lifted a notch. She'd managed to get her way and not make an enemy. It was always good to have a "friend" among the people she was studying.

A couple of steps from Flint Collins's closed door, she stopped. That damned baby cry was going off again. She didn't want to interrupt his call. Nor did she want to wait around while he talked on the phone.

And really, what kind of guy had a crying newborn as his ringtone?

Not one she'd ever want to associate with, that was for sure.

However she didn't want to get on the guy's bad side. Not yet, anyway. She needed him to like her. To trust her.

She might even need to learn about his life if she hoped to help her father. According to Bill, anyway. The director was pretty certain that Collins wouldn't have hidden anything he was doing in files to which she'd have access.

The crying had stopped. She didn't hear any voices. Had whoever was calling hung up?

Deciding to wait a couple of seconds, just in case he was listening to a caller on the other end, Tamara cringed as the baby cry started back up. Sounding painfully realistic. How could he stand that?

Apparently he'd let the call go to voice mail. And whoever had been at the other end was phoning back. Was Collins ignoring the call? Unless he wasn't there? Had he left his cell in his office?

A man like Flint Collins didn't leave his cell phone behind.

Tamara knocked. And when there was no answer, tried the door. Surprisingly the knob turned. The office was impressive. Neat. Classy. Elegant.

And had nothing on the spread of male shoulders she saw bending over something to the side of his desk. Or the backside beneath them.

"Why aren't you answering your phone?" she blurted. The crying had to stop. It was making her crazy. She had business to do with him and—

The way those shoulders jerked and his glance swung in her direction clearly indicated that he hadn't heard her enter. Making her uncomfortably aware that she should probably have knocked a second time.

How hadn't he heard her first knock?

The thought fled as soon as she realized that the crying was coming from closer to him. There by the window. Not from the cell phone she noticed on his desk as she approached.

And then she saw it…the carrier…on the chair next to him. He'd been rocking it.

"What on earth are you doing to that baby?" she exclaimed, nothing in mind but to rescue the child in obvious distress. To stop the noise that was going to send her spiraling if she wasn't careful.

"Damned if I know," he said loudly enough to be heard over the noise. "I fed her, burped her, changed her. I've done everything they said to do, but she won't stop crying."

Tamara was already unbuckling the strap that held the crying infant in her seat. She was so tiny! Couldn't have been more than a few days old. Her skin was still wrinkled and so, so red. There were no tears on her cheeks.

"There's nothing poking her. I checked," Collins said, not interfering as she lifted the baby from the seat, careful to support the little head.

It wasn't until that warm weight settled against her that Tamara realized what she'd done. She was holding a baby. Something she couldn't do.

She was going to pay. With a hellacious nightmare at the very least.

The baby's cries had stopped as soon as Tamara picked her up.

"What did you do?" Collins was there, practically touching her, he was standing so close.

"Nothing. I picked her up."

"There must've been some problem with the seat, after all…" He'd tossed the infant head support on the desk and was removing the washable cover.

"I'm guessing she just wanted to be held," Tamara said. What the hell was she doing?

Tearless crying generally meant anger, not physical distress.

And why did Flint Collins have a baby in his office?

She had to put the child down. But couldn't until he put the seat back together. The newborn's eyes were closed and she hiccuped and then sighed.

Clenching her lips for a second, Tamara looked away. "Babies need to be held almost as much as they need to be fed," she told him while she tried to understand what was going on. "The skin-to-skin contact, the cuddling, is vitally important not only to their current emotional well-being but to future emotional, developmental and social behavior."

She was quoting books she'd memorized—long ago— in another life. He was checking the foam beneath the seat cover and the straps, too. Her initial analysis indicated that he was fairly distraught himself.

Not what she would've predicted from a hard-core businessman possibly stealing from her father.

"Who is she?" she asked, figuring it was best to start at the bottom and work her way up to exposing him for the thief he probably was.

He straightened. Stared at the baby in her arms, his brown eyes softening and yet giving away a hint of what looked like fear at the same time. In that second she wished like hell that her father was wrong and Collins wouldn't turn out to be the one who was stealing from Owens Investments.

She didn't move. Just stood frozen with her arms holding a baby against her.

"Her name's Diamond Rose." His tone soft, he continued to watch the baby, as though he couldn't look away. But he had to get that seat dealt with. Fast. The lump in her throat grew.

"Whose is she?" She was going to have to put the baby down. Sooner rather than later. Her permanently broken heart couldn't take much more. The tears were already starting to build. Dammit! She'd gone almost two months without them.

"Mine...sort of."

Her head shot up. "Yours?" She glanced at the cell phone on his desk and then noticed the portable baby monitor. "You don't have a baby crying ringtone?"

"No."

"You have a baby?"

There'd been nothing in his file. According to her father, he'd only been dating his current girlfriend—some high-powered attorney—for the past six months. He'd brought her to a dinner Howard had hosted for top producers and their significant others. And had explained where and how they'd met. Which was pertinent because soon after he'd taken the first full vacation he'd had in eight years.

"She's not mine," he said then frowned, glancing at Tamara hesitantly before holding her gaze. "Legally, she is. But I'm not her father."

"Who is?" His personnel records hadn't listed any next of kin other than an incarcerated mother.

He shrugged. "That's the six-million-dollar question. No idea. Biologically she's my sister."

Tamara flooded with emotion. She couldn't swallow. Standing completely still, concentrating on distancing herself from the deluge, focusing on him, she waited for her skin to cool. With a warm baby snuggled against her chest.

She had to get rid of that warmth.

Get away from the baby.

"Your mother had a baby?" she heard herself ask, sounding only a little squeaky.

He nodded.

"I thought she was in prison…" She suddenly realized she might have revealed too much. She was being too invasive for a first business meeting. "Um, Bill told me. He said you'd overcome a…difficult past."

He nodded. "She was. And the fact that she was a convict makes the question about Diamond's father that much harder to answer. Who's going to admit to fathering a child illegally?"

Her nerves were quaking. "She gave birth in prison?"

"Three days ago."

She'd been right. The child was only days old…

Days older than any of hers had lived to be.

"And she gave her to you?" She wasn't going to be able to keep it together much longer.

He'd agreed to take a baby. That said something about him. He needed to take her from Tamara.

He'd taken on a child. But then, his mother, a criminal, had agreed to take him on, too. By birthing him. Keeping him.

"My mother died in childbirth."

Flint's shocking words hit her harder than they would

have if she'd been on the other side of the room. Or in another room. Speaking to him on the phone.

Knees starting to feel weak, she knew she was out of time. "And just like that, you become a father?"

"Just like that."

There were things she should say. More questions to ask. But Tamara simply stood there, staring at him.

Unable to move.

To speak.

She was shaking visibly.

And had to get rid of the bundle she held.

Pronto.

## Chapter Five

"Here, you need to take her."

As the pink-wrapped bundle came toward him with more speed than he would've expected, Flint reached out automatically, allowing the baby's head to glide up to his elbow, her body settling on his lower arm. While holding a baby was still foreign to him, he was beginning to notice a rhythm, a sense of having done it before.

"She needs to bond with you." The woman was a stranger to him and yet she was sharing one of the most intimate experiences in his life. His coming to grips with a reality he had little idea how to deal with and a role he was unsure of. Burying his mother. Meeting his sister. Becoming for all intents and purposes, a father. All happening in one day. He'd been about to lose it—and she'd saved him.

Just like she'd saved him from almost certain job loss earlier.

Could she really be, somehow, heaven-sent? By his

mother, not any divine source watching out for him. He'd long ago ceased hoping for that one.

Did he dare even think of his mother making it to an afterlife that would allow her to help her baby girl?

Was he losing his damned mind?

"Until two days ago, I didn't know the first thing about children." He hardly remembered being one. It seemed to him he'd grown up as an adult. "Babies in particular."

"You've had her for two days?" The woman had backed up to the other side of the desk and was halfway to the door. A couple of times she'd rubbed her hands along shapely thighs covered by a deliciously short skirt and was now clasping them together as though, at any second, they might fly apart.

"I just got her today," he said, calming a bit now as the baby settled against him as easily as she had with the efficiency expert. It was the first time he'd actually held the infant.

All he'd done so far was pick her up to lay her on a pad on the table. And to put her back in her carrier to feed her. That was it.

"So, how often does the holding thing need to happen?" How far behind was he?

"All the time." She was nodding, as though following the beat of some song in her head. Rubbed her thighs again, then was wringing her hands. Then reached for the door-knob. "When you're feeding her, certainly, and other times, too. Whenever you can. There are, um, books, classes and, you know, places you can go to learn everything…"

"I spent the weekend crash coursing. I guess I zoned out on the holding part."

"Parents holding their babies is a…biological imperative. They can't get enough of it. The babies, I mean. And…"

She turned away as though she couldn't wait to escape. Which made no sense to him, considering how naturally she'd rescued Diamond Rose from his inept attempts to "parent" her.

"What did you want?" His question was blunt but he wasn't ready for her to go. Not until his baby sister had a few more minutes with him—while he still had the efficiency expert's child-care guidance. To make sure Diamond was satisfied, for now, with what he could do for her.

"Um…oh, it can wait."

She glanced at the baby again, her eyes lingering this time. And then she seemed unusually interested in the wall on the opposite side of the room.

"Seriously. You needed something from me. I'm here to work." He couldn't afford to be a problem, considering how badly he needed this job.

The expert took a step away from the door and he waited for the business discussion to start. Tried not to pay attention to how beautiful she was. Like no woman he'd ever encountered before. A compelling combination of business savvy, sexy, glamorous and natural, too.

He thought her name was Tamara, but wasn't positive he was remembering correctly. He'd been a bit distracted when they'd met earlier.

But if he could get her to put in a good word with Howard on his behalf…

"I'm sorry about your mother." She sounded a little less harassed.

He nodded. Settled his bundle a little more securely against him.

She stared at the crook of his arm, then looked around the office. Seemed to spy the Pack 'n Play still in its box tucked away by the long curtain on the far window. "I guess you haven't had time to make child-care arrangements."

Efficiency expert. Finding a problem with his efficiency?

"I sold three thousand shares at 475 percent of their purchased value today." He'd made an outrageous amount of money for a client who liked to take risks. And a hefty sum for the brokerage, though it wasn't an investment Howard would have approved of because of the risk. He could just as easily have lost the entire sum.

The efficiency expert blinked. Gave her head a little shake. Drawing his attention to the auburn curls falling around her shoulders.

"I…asked about child care?" She sounded as though she was doubting his mental faculties now. She could join the club. If ever a man had lost it, that was him.

"Because if you need help, I know someone…"

*Oh.*

"I need to find out if I have a job first," he told her. Bill hadn't fired him. But he hadn't said his job was secure, either. Flint hadn't heard from him all afternoon. Or from Howard.

Either of them could have seen the sale he'd made, with their access to the company's portfolios. He assumed they both had. They were that kind of businessmen. Always on top of what mattered.

Which was why he was working there.

"Were you intending to open your own business? I heard Mr. Coniff ask about that as I approached his officer earlier."

Not an efficiency-related question. But it was a human one. He was standing there, holding a baby, and had just told her, before he'd made anyone else in the company aware, that the child was suddenly his.

And that he'd lost his mother.

He'd also told her that he wasn't sure he still had a job.

"Yes, I was in the process of opening my own business." No point in denying the truth. Lying wasn't his way. "I intended to tell Howard as soon as the final paperwork was in order."

"And now you aren't?"

Diamond Rose sighed. He felt that breath as if he'd taken it himself. "Starting a new business, especially in this field, takes an eighteen-hour-a-day commitment and comes with more than average financial risk. I can no longer afford the time or the risk."

"Because of the baby."

Because he had no idea how to be a father. He had to learn. "I'm her only family."

She nodded, looking at him, meeting his gaze. Not glancing, even occasionally, at his baby sister. She wasn't wringing her hands anymore, either, which he considered to be a good thing.

Still…

"Howard doesn't know about her yet. I didn't actually see her myself until this morning. I'd appreciate it if you'd give me a little time to get my act together before you say anything."

"I work for him," she said. And then, "How much time?"

He calculated…between the month he'd probably need and the minute or two she seemed willing to give him. "Twenty-four hours, max."

She watched him.

"I've got sixty times that in vacation days coming to me." From an efficiency standpoint, she wouldn't be risking anything. He could certainly ask for twenty-four hours.

"But you…didn't take today off."

"I rarely take time off. And I had stocks I had to sell or risk a big loss."

He'd had all the losses he could handle. His mother. His fiancée. His business. All at once. In the past couple of days. Astonishing that he was still standing there.

Except that he'd had no choice. Someone had to take care of his mother's brand-new baby.

Tamara—yes, that was definitely her name, Tamara Frost—was silent. A few long seconds later she said, "I see no harm in allowing you the time to go to your boss yourself."

He could have kissed her. He shook off the feeling. He'd just met the woman! Whether or not she was his mother's way of helping him from the great beyond, he had no time— and no mental or emotional capacity—to engage in any kind of liaison.

Yet he clung to the idea of having her on his side.

"Thank you."

"So…you just got her this morning? And came straight here?" She sounded a bit incredulous.

"I had stocks I had to sell," he repeated. A job to save. He couldn't afford a big loss on top of everything else. That much he knew. He needed Howard Owens to need him around; he certainly didn't want to give the older man more reason to fire him.

Her expression changed. Softened, although she hadn't looked at the baby again. Not in a while. "I'd like to give you the name of a friend of mine. She runs a day care not far from here. Most places don't take infants younger than six weeks, but considering your circumstances, I'm pretty sure she'd make an exception. I promise you, you won't be sorry. She treats the children in her care like they're her own. Gets to know them. Loves them. Babies get dedicated holding time. She takes everything that happens to her kids personally."

He wasn't ready to pass off his bundle to a stranger. Not out of his sight, at least.

Ms. Frost had given him twenty-four hours to report to Howard with some kind of baby management plan—well, to report to Howard that he had a child. Having the plan was his own stipulation.

"Does she watch your children?" Tamara wasn't wearing a ring, but she'd been such a natural with Diamond Rose... Seemed to know everything about babies...

A shadow passed over Tamara's face. He pretended not to notice. But when you knew the depth of sorrow yourself, you noticed.

"I don't have children. My work is my life. My job requires a lot of travel. It's not as if companies can come to me! And I don't think it's right to have children and then not be there to raise them. I love what I do, so I made a conscious choice."

Then why the shadow in her eyes?

And what business was that of his?

Particularly since he already owed her so much. She'd interrupted at exactly the right time that morning, preventing him from losing his job, at least temporarily.

Giving him time to close the deal he'd opened at the end of the prior week. To make his company so much money, it would be harder to fire him.

She'd agreed he could have time to come up with a plan to present to Howard regarding his changed life status. A way to convince him that in spite of everything that had happened, he was still a smart business risk.

And she was the expert Howard had just hired—meaning Howard most likely trusted her implicitly. If Flint could stay on her good side...

"I'd appreciate your friend's information," he said. He nodded to a pad and pen on his desk that she could use to write down the woman's name and phone number. All the while, he held the sleeping newborn between his left arm and body.

He could do this. Work. Take care of business. And a baby.

As long as his baby sister didn't cry again. He'd hold her. Feed her. Burp her. Change her. And hold her again. How hard could it be?

"I'll leave you to it, then…"

Momentary panic flared as Tamara Frost walked back to the door of his office. "Wait!"

She turned.

"You… What did you want? Initially?" She couldn't have come to give him her friend's number. She hadn't known he had a baby. "When you knocked at my door?"

"I'm going to be conducting interviews with all department heads, with all top producers and with some randomly chosen office staff throughout the next week or so. I stopped by to set up an appointment to meet with you. But clearly you need to get your ship in order before I climb aboard."

She was smooth. All business. If he hadn't already been attracted to her, he'd have fallen right then. He wasn't going to start anything—or even think about it. But he couldn't help his reaction and was smart enough to acknowledge it to himself. Rather that than have it club him over the head at some point. Now *that*, he couldn't afford.

Reminding himself he'd decided to stay on her good side, to shield his position with Howard, he sent her a smile reserved for his best clients. "Whatever works for you," he told her. "I'll make myself available." Career came first with him.

The bundle in his arms blew a loud fart.

He'd forgotten, for a brief second, that he was no longer the man he'd been.

"Talk to Mallory," Tamara said, referring to the friend whose number she'd written down. "Talk to Howard. And then give me a call."

"I don't have your number."

"It's in the email sent to everyone this morning."

It was late afternoon and he'd yet to read any company-related mail. He'd handled his clients' correspondence, though. Made all his phone calls. Set up a couple of important lunches for later in the week.

Flint would have come up with some charming, pithy response if the expert had waited a little longer. Apparently she was too efficient for that.

Watching the door close behind her, he glanced at the baby in his arms and felt...weak.

The boy who'd been resilient enough to get on a school bus as a runt kindergartener and sit among the bullies wasn't sure how he was going to proceed through the next hour.

## Chapter Six

Tamara canceled dinner with her parents two hours after she'd accepted her mother's invitation. Dr. Sheila Owens had reached her after rounds that afternoon, thrilled that Howard had finally spoken with Tamara about his business problems and that she was already at work, trying to find the thief who was stealing from them. Sheila had wanted them to meet as a family and talk about the issue.

Tamara decided her best efforts would be spent poring over files instead. To begin with, eight years' worth of Flint Collins's investments transactions.

First, though, she'd suggested to her father that someone get Collins to sign that noncompete clause and let him know he wasn't on the brink of being fired. Half an hour later she received a call from him, saying that Collins had just come out of Bill Coniff's office and that Coniff had the signed form in his possession. Smiling as she hung up, she was satisfied with her day's work.

And happier than she should be to know that the man she'd so recently met was no longer worrying about being gainfully employed. Flint Collins had enough to deal with at the moment. .

She couldn't go soft on him, though. That was how a lot of white-collar criminals succeeded in their fraudulent efforts. By charming those around them, winning the trust of those they were cheating.

At the same time, the guy was human, not yet proved guilty of anything other than wanting to branch out on his own, and deserving of some compassion on the day he'd buried his mother.

She looked away from the computer screen in her compact new office on the third floor of the building her father owned. She had a feeling it had been a big storage closet of some kind prior to being hastily converted for her. Howard knew better than to lay down the red carpet for a paid consultant he supposedly didn't know other than by reputation.

At least the room was private.

She'd had worse in the two years she'd been on the road.

A window would have been nice.

Oh, God… That baby…

Glancing at the time in the corner of her computer screen, she picked up the phone. She'd left one message for Mallory. But it was five o'clock now. Most of the children would have been picked up. And Flint Collins would be calling, if he hadn't already.

She needed to speak with her friend.

"I was about to call you," Mallory said when she answered. "I got your message, and I have one from Mr. Collins, too. He needs to speak with me by tomorrow afternoon, he said."

She'd given him a deadline to talk to her father. Not that

he had to have day care arranged before letting his bosses know that he'd just become a father. Of sorts.

"So you haven't spoken with him?"

"No, your message said I should talk to you first."

Tamara nodded. She thought she'd asked that but couldn't be sure. She'd been a bit off her mark when she'd made the call, having come directly from Flint Collins's office.

Where she'd had a newborn baby snuggled against her chest.

A chill swept through her and her insides started to quake again. Until she focused on the computer screen. The rows of numbers she'd been studying.

It was all about focus.

When she could feel the bands around her chest loosening, she told Mallory about Flint Collins suddenly finding himself the sole caregiver of a newborn baby. She didn't include the personal details. That was for him to share, or not, as he chose. His personal situation wasn't why she was calling.

"I held the baby, Mal," she said in the very next breath. "I was in his office and I didn't know she was there. I heard her cry and saw that he was just standing there, in front of her carrier. Maybe he was rocking it or something, I don't know. But without thinking I went right up and unstrapped her and picked her up."

The silence on the other end of the line wasn't a surprise. Mallory's calm tone when she said, "What happened next?" was different than Tamara had expected.

Only a handful of people knew the true extent of her struggles, how close she'd come to thinking she'd never have another happy moment. Mallory was one of them.

Because Mallory had been there, too, a few years before. They'd met in a small counseling group designed solely for young mothers who'd lost a baby.

"I started to unravel," she admitted. "Not as quickly as I would've expected, but I was working and it took a while for that barrier to break down."

She could feel the bands tightening around her lungs again. Her entire chest. Her ribs. Physical manifestations of the panic she fought, less often now, but still regularly enough that she'd stayed in touch with her support group.

"So, basically, you held it together."

"On the surface."

Their psychiatrist had offered them all medications, individually, of course. She and Mallory had preferred not to depend on drugs and opted to fight the battle on their own. And because neither one of them had ever remotely considered actually taking her own life—on the contrary, they'd both been in possession of enough equilibrium to maintain careers—they'd been left to their decisions without undue pressure.

"And what about now? How do you feel?"

They were supposed to be talking about Flint. And that...needy little child.

"Like I want a glass of wine and a jet to someplace far, far away." She had to be honest. It was the only way to succeed on her personal survival mission. "I've got the jitters, my hands are sweaty on and off."

She'd had hot and cold flashes, too, but didn't mention them. They didn't have anything to do with the infant. Although, come to think of it, both had happened in the presence of Flint Collins. During the first, though, they'd been in Bill Coniff's office and she hadn't known Flint was a new dad. She'd thought she had the flu, but no other symptoms had developed.

She was so busy convincing herself that the hot and

cold flashes, something new in her panic world, had nothing to do with the baby, that she'd walked herself right into another mental trap. Were the flashes because of *Flint*? Because of how incredibly attractive he was? Like, Hollywood ad attractive?

Was she *physically* reacting to him? As in being inordinately turned on?

No. Tamara shook her head. *Don't borrow trouble*, she told herself.

"What's wrong?" she asked when she realized Mallory hadn't responded to her list of symptoms.

"I was hoping…"

She knew what Mallory would've been hoping. They'd had the discussion. Many times.

Now they'd had the experiment Mallory had begged for and Tamara had always point-blank refused.

*She'd held a baby.* It had been horrible.

"Absolutely not." She made her point quite clear. "Never again."

"Maybe because you were so convinced it was a bad thing…" Mallory, bless her heart, refused to give up.

Tamara had nothing more to say on the subject.

"It works, Tamara, I swear to you. If you'd just try. Give it a chance. I'm living proof, every single day. If you knew how much healthier I am… How much happier… How much stronger…"

She'd only met Mallory after the other woman's infant son had died, yet Tamara knew her well enough now to be certain that Mallory had always had a core of strength.

"I get comfort from them—real, lasting comfort— knowing that little ones are on this earth, healthy and robust and happy and full of love."

"I know you do." And it wasn't that Tamara didn't want

a world filled with healthy, robust, loving babies. She did. Very much. She just couldn't have them in *her* world.

Because her heart knew the pain of four babies who hadn't been healthy enough to make it into the world alive. She knew the pain of losing a baby that everyone had thought was healthy. It happened. Babies died. In the womb and out of it, too. She'd survived losing Ryan. Barely. She couldn't afford the risk of another bout of that kind of pain and the residual depression.

"I'm not you," she said now, aware that it wasn't what Mallory wanted to hear.

Silence hung on the line again. But not as long this time.

"So tell me about this guy you referred. Flint Collins? You said I should speak with you first…" Her voice trailed off in midsentence and then Mallory continued. "Or was that it? It was about how you felt when you held his baby?"

"No." She'd had hot flashes both times she'd been with Flint. Not just because of his looks. He was confident, capable, successful—and had chosen to give up his business dream to care for a sister he hadn't even known he had. He had a baby who desperately needed a mother. He'd be a great match for Mallory.

She shook her head. No, he had a girlfriend. And besides…

"I need your word that what I'm about to tell you stays between you and me. Period. No one else."

"Of course. I assumed everything we told each other was that way. The two of us—our conversations are like an extension of being in session, right?"

The tone of voice… Tamara could picture the vulnerable look that would be shining from Mallory's soft blue eyes.

"Right," she said. "I just… This isn't about us and I needed to make certain…"

"You and me, our friendship—we're sacred," Mallory said, her voice gaining strength.

"Okay, good." Tamara took the first easy breath she'd had since she'd stepped into Flint's office. "I found out today why my mom and dad wanted me home so badly. Dad needs my help at Owens Investments. Someone's stealing from him and he suspects it might be Flint Collins. I'm working as an efficiency expert for him as a cover so I can have access to all the company files and employees, to stick my nose anywhere I want, to see if I can find some kind of proof for Dad to take to the police."

"Why doesn't he hire a detective?"

"Because right now only his accountant knows. If word gets out that there's something untrustworthy going on in the company, his investors will take off like birds flying south for the winter."

"How sure is he that Collins is his guy?"

"The evidence is stacked against him at the moment. But it's all hearsay and circumstantial."

"And he's a new dad?"

"I'll let him fill you in on the details. But, Mal? Whatever he's doing in his business life, this baby… She's only three days old. If ever a baby needed you, it's her. Even more so if it turns out her dad's involved in criminal activity. I felt you had to know, in case something comes down and there's some reflection on your business."

Not too long ago, a woman had showed up at Mallory's day care claiming that one of the kids was the woman's two-year-old son, who'd been kidnapped. Things had been rough going there for several weeks. And then the woman's story turned out to be true. That had all taken place before Tamara had returned from Boston, but she'd heard about it over the phone.

"No one can blame a newborn baby for anything. But I'll be careful not to let him see the books," she said with a chuckle.

Tamara smiled, too. An easy smile. One that felt natural. Her breath came more easily, too. She'd known she could count on Mallory.

And maybe, if Flint wasn't the thief, he and Mallory could make a family for that precious baby—

No, he had a girlfriend. Some powerful lawyer.

Because he was hedging all his bets as a smart investor would? In case he needed a top-notch lawyer?

She couldn't help wondering, as she ended her call with Mallory, what that rich girlfriend, who'd apparently been responsible for a change in Flint's spending habits, or at least his driving and vacation habits, thought of having a convict's baby to raise?

And then berated herself for being so catty.

The other woman was probably perfectly wonderful. She might already be making plans for the baby's care and Flint had just taken Mallory's contact information to give them options.

In any case, it was none of her business.

Yes, she thought again. Flint Collins and his new life were absolutely none of her business. She'd simply been the one to walk in on his intense day.

She looked back at her computer screen.

*Focus.* That was all it took. Focus.

## Chapter Seven

*"Bathing your newborn baby with the umbilical cord stump still attached is fine,"* the pediatrician in the video confirmed. *"There is no great risk that the stump will get infected. Take care to make sure that the area is thoroughly dried."*

Holding his sleeping sister in the crook of one arm, Flint paused his continued scouring of articles and videos on the internet—all from verified, legitimate pediatric sources and nationally recognized clinics and associations. He found this video particularly informative, considering his current dilemma.

*"It is not necessary to bathe your baby every day,"* she continued. *"Up to three times a week, for the first year, is fine. As long as you're quick and thorough with diaper changes and burp cloths, you're cleaning the critical areas often enough. Daily bathing is not recommended, since it can dry out the baby's skin."*

Okay. Good. He didn't have to deal with a bath his first night. Her first night with him.

He could have hired a nurse to help out with this transition stage, but hadn't really even considered doing so. He'd always taken care of himself—and his mother when he could. He'd take care of Diamond, too. The baby wasn't going to be shoved off on strangers anytime that he was available to care for her. As he'd been so many times.

"Dodged a bullet on that one, Diamond Rose," he said, glancing at the sleeping baby. He'd been doing that a lot, all day. Glancing at her. He'd even caught himself staring at her a time or two.

It was just so hard to believe she was there. His flesh and blood.

A rush of love he couldn't have imagined swamped him. He acknowledged it. And moved on. He'd learned a long time ago to move on when it came to those kinds of emotions.

A guy had to cope, to push forward. To accomplish.

*"It's best to use a small plastic tub, or a kitchen sink, when bathing a newborn..."*

Clicking to open an additional browser window, he shopped for plastic tubs. Found one at the local children's store he'd spent bundles in that weekend. How had he missed the tub aisle? He added it to the shopping list he'd made for the following day.

And thought about Tamara Frost. Wondering what she was doing. If she had a significant other and was with him. She hadn't been wearing a wedding ring, but that didn't necessarily mean anything these days.

He wondered how she'd react if he gave in to the urge that had been nagging at him most of the evening and called her.

Before he'd figured out his immediate plans. Before speaking with Howard as she'd instructed.

He'd spoken with Mallory Harris and had an arrangement to meet with her the following day, time to be determined.

First priority was Howard Owens. He'd sent off an email that afternoon, requesting an in-person meeting as soon as possible. Once he heard back, he'd schedule—or reschedule—everything else.

He checked his email again. No response yet.

Nothing from Stella, either, not that he'd expected anything. She'd made her feelings perfectly clear. The baby or her. His choice was in his arms, breathing against him.

Maybe he should be missing Stella more than he was, or at least be hurting… Maybe he would at some point. There just wasn't room enough right now. His capacity for grief was taken up with Alana Gold.

The woman who'd taught him a long time ago that no matter how much he loved her, it wouldn't be enough to keep her home with him. Not forever.

Having Stella in his life had been wonderful. And yet part of him had always believed it wouldn't last.

Glancing at the clock, Flint figured he had another hour and fifteen minutes before he'd need to measure formula, heat, change, feed and burp again. Adjusting the baby so she was lying against him, propped in the curve of his body, and freeing enough of his left arm to allow him to type, he clicked on the most used site on his browser's favorite bar—the stock exchange.

Twelve-eleven a.m.

One-oh-six a.m.

One fifty-two a.m.

Wiping the tears from her cheeks, Tamara sat up in

bed. Turning on the bedside lamp she'd purchased from an antiques mall before she'd moved east, she pulled her laptop off the nightstand and flipped it open—the third time since she'd gone to bed that she'd done it.

She'd focus. Work until she couldn't keep her eyes open. And then she'd sleep. Until she woke up shaking again.

The nightmares weren't the same. But they all *felt* identical. Sometimes she'd be holding Ryan, feeling so incredibly happy. Complete. And then she'd wake and the devastating loss would be as fresh now as though she was feeling it for the first time.

She didn't completely hate that dream. Those moments holding her baby—they were almost worth waking up for.

That night they were the other kind. The ones where she wasn't even around children at all. She'd be someplace—sometimes she recognized it, sometimes she didn't—and she couldn't get out. It could be a maze. A building. A hole in the ground.

Sometimes she'd be on a path in the dark with so many obstacles she couldn't move.

She'd hear a cry. Someone needing her. And she could never get to whoever it was.

Or she'd reach the end of the path and there'd be a dead baby. Wrapped in a beautiful blanket. Always wrapped in that blanket.

Once there'd been an empty casket.

In the beginning she'd been inside her own womb multiple times. Trapped. Unable to get out.

She'd had that dream again tonight. Before the 1:52 a.m. wakening. Which was why she was sitting up.

She could take a sleeping pill. Knock herself out.

The thought gave her comfort. Knowing she wasn't going to do it gave her determination.

Focus gave her peace.

Damn Flint Collins. Bringing his newborn baby sister to work. She wasn't going to think about him, other than to dissect his dealings with Owens Investments down to the last cent. Every investment. Every sale. Every client. Every expense report. Every report he ever wrote, period.

How his first night with a brand-new baby was going was not her concern.

The vulnerable look in those dark brown eyes didn't mean he wasn't guilty of theft.

The baby resting against that gorgeous, suited torso had no bearing on his business dealings.

Tamara was not going to have a relapse.

She was going to focus.

Setting his phone to wake him every two hours, knowing he was going to be up several times during the night, Flint had considered himself fully prepared for his first night as a brother/father. Or at least his first night as the sole responsible person for his "inheritance."

When at 1:52 a.m. he was up for the fourth time, holding a bottle to a sleeping baby's mouth, he didn't feel capable of anything more. She'd cry. He'd feed her. She'd fall asleep sucking on the nipple. He'd put her back to bed and within half an hour her cry would sound on the monitor again, waking him.

At a little after one, he'd let her cry. She wasn't due for another feeding until two thirty. She was dry. Surely she'd fall back asleep.

She hadn't.

He'd changed her Pack 'n Play sheet.

He'd changed her diaper, even though she'd been completely dry.

He'd checked the stump of her umbilical cord.

And used the axillary thermometer under her arm. It had registered perfectly normal.

So he'd put the bottle back in her mouth and she'd sucked and swallowed for a few minutes before going back to sleep.

He hadn't heard from Howard Owens. Had Tamara put in a good word for him? Or broken her promise and told his CEO that Flint had a crying baby in his office?

Even if he heard from Howard first thing, inviting him up, how sharp was he going to be in the morning on less than two hours' sleep?

He had to get some rest. Parents didn't stop requiring sleep the second they had a kid. His mom had slept.

Not that his mother was the greatest role model but, in this case, the thought made sense.

Settling the baby in her Pack 'n Play, double-checking the monitor, he quietly crossed the hall to his room, slid between the sheets and closed his eyes.

A vision of Tamara Frost was there. Her fiery hair, a cross between brown and red, curling and long, framing the gold-rimmed green eyes...

His eyes open, he stared at the ceiling for a couple of seconds before closing them again. He was supposed to be resting, not getting turned on.

Memories of the gravesite that morning assailed him. And then Bill Coniff's distrusting face when Flint had asked for job security.

The sale he'd made had been a success. He had a client for life on that one. And earned his job security, as it had turned out.

He'd signed the noncompete. Financially he was sound.

Careerwise, he'd still be doing what he was good at.

Tamara Frost wanted a sit-down with him—

The monitor beside him blew that thought away.

Diamond Rose was awake again. Desperate now, he picked her up, wasn't even surprised when she quit crying the second he was holding her. With his free hand, he hauled her portable playpen into his room. It wasn't what he'd planned, but it now seemed the only sensible choice.

The playpen went right next to the bed, He placed the baby inside while she was still awake, talking to her the whole time, then lay down beside her, keeping his hand on the netted side of the crib.

"I'm right here, Little One," he said. "Right here. I'm always going to be right here. For as long as I live. That's the one thing you can count on. And I'm going to give it to you straight, too. That's what I do. Mom always said I was going to *be* someone."

He paused, thinking that last statement highly inappropriate. Stupid, even. Diamond Rose's eyes half blinked open.

"We'll get better at this." He started talking again immediately. "We'll figure it out together. No—scratch that. *You're* great. I'll get better. *I'll* figure it out. You go ahead and be a newborn. And then someday you'll be a kid, and I'll still be here, still figuring things out. You won't need to start doing that until you're at least ten. Maybe twenty. Yeah, twenty works. We'll revisit it when you're twenty and see where we're at…"

The baby was zonked. But just for good measure, Flint kept right on telling her how it was going to be until he'd talked himself to sleep.

How could a woman accomplish the tasks before her if the people in her life insisted on pulling her into distractions she could ill afford?

Hating the thought, retracting it immediately, Tamara

picked up the phone when she saw Flint Collins's name pop up.

Yeah, she'd added him to her contacts. Because she'd given him her number and if he was calling, she wanted a warning before she picked up.

"Hello, this is Tamara," she said in her most professional voice.

"I'm available to meet with you at your earliest convenience."

"I'm sorry, who is this?"

"Flint. Collins. You asked me to phone to set up a meeting after I met with Howard Owens. I'm calling to let you know I've done that."

His voice, all masculine confidence, didn't sound like he was reporting anything—and shouldn't be sending chills all the way through her.

"Yes, Mr. Collins. I've got meetings scheduled all day today. Let me see where I can fit you in."

She hadn't scheduled even one yet. She had people waiting to hear on times. She'd been waiting on him. Because, at the moment, her father didn't give a damn about the efficiency of his staff.

"You've met with Mr. Owens already today?" she asked inanely, buying herself a moment to cool down. She knew he had, and not just because he'd told her so. She'd had a call from her father the minute Flint Collins had left his office.

Just as she'd had a call from Mallory earlier that morning, the second she'd had Diamond Rose in her care. For the first time ever Tamara had almost had to ask her friend to stop talking. The way Mallory had gushed over the baby, thanking her for the chance to help care for the motherless infant. And then stating again that she couldn't believe the baby hadn't worked her magic on Tamara.

That had been right about the time Tamara had begun second-guessing the wisdom of her decision in sending Flint to Mallory.

But she'd quickly recovered. She'd made the right choice for Diamond Rose, first. And for Mallory, too.

Flint Collins was still on the line, having told her that not only had he met with her father, but that Howard Owens had been completely decent about everything— about keeping him on and the fact that he suddenly had sole care of an infant.

There it was again. *Sole care*. Her father had told her the same thing, adding that he'd suggested Flint take a few weeks off to get acclimated to this major change in his life. Flint had demurred, saying he already had care plans in effect for the infant. Tamara had wanted to ask about the lawyer girlfriend her father had mentioned the day before—clarifying that "sole care" meant that Flint was the child's only guardian, for now. But she hadn't actually voiced the question.

She still didn't know why she'd hesitated. Just that bringing up Collins's girlfriend to her father had seemed… uncomfortable.

Which made no sense at all.

She looked around her small office. And pictured his, which would undoubtedly still have the baby smell. Or at least her memory of it. "Can you do lunch?" she finished.

Yes, a nice public meeting. Over food. Something to do while she questioned him about…she wasn't sure what. So far, the figures that had put her to sleep the night before were all adding up, and all looked legitimate.

What she needed to see was his personal bank account. His personal tax records.

She had no access to either.

"Lunch would be fine," Flint said, suggesting a place

that she recognized. Close to the office but more upscale than they needed. A third-floor place down by the pier, overlooking the ocean.

She needed him fully cooperative—willing to give her the goods on himself when she didn't even know where to look—so she graciously accepted. Agreed to meet him in the lobby to walk the short distance between her father's building and the restaurant.

Although it was the first of November, San Diego was San Diego, no matter what season it was. She wouldn't be cold in her navy formfitting dress pants and short navy jacket. And the wedged shoes… Having worn five-inch heels more times than she could count, she figured she could walk in pretty much anything.

She just hoped she wasn't walking *into* something that would turn out to be more than she could handle.

Her father was counting on her.

## Chapter Eight

She never should have agreed to walk over to the restaurant with him. While the day was pleasant, and being out in the sun with the blue skies overhead was even better—especially considering the windowless room where she'd spent her morning—Tamara still regretted her choice. The people milling around them, tourists lollygagging and business people bustling, left her and Flint Collins in a world of their own.

At least that was how it felt to her.

While people could probably hear what they said, with everyone moving at a different pace, no one could follow their conversation.

Making their togetherness seem too personal. Too intimate.

To begin with, they just talked about being hungry. About the restaurant. They'd both been there many times.

She liked their grilled chicken salad. He was planning on the grilled chicken and jalapeño ciabatta.

It didn't surprise her that he was a daring eater. Preferred his food hot.

The crowds forced them closer together than she would've liked. At one point he put a hand at her back to lead her ahead of him as they crossed the street.

He didn't touch her, exactly, but she could feel the heat of his presence.

Looking down, she could see the tips of his shining black shoes and the hem of the dark gray business pants he was wearing with a white shirt and red power tie.

New baby or not, he'd been perfectly and professionally put together when he'd greeted her in the lobby earlier. She hadn't asked about Diamond Rose. If she wanted to get closer to him for the sake of her father's investigation, she probably should ask—

"You mentioned that you travel all over the country to the companies you work for, like Owens Investments, yet you seem so familiar with the area. Are you staying nearby?"

"I was born and raised in San Diego." She didn't see any harm in telling him that. "I work locally as much as I can, but I need to be free to go where the jobs take me."

At least that was the plan—to work locally as often as possible. She'd only started to send out her portfolio to companies in the area. She'd always gone where she'd been sent, but she wasn't with a big firm anymore. She was on her own and would be responsible for finding her own work.

As soon as she finished the job she was on.

She'd spoken with her father again, just before leaving for lunch. She'd been through every line item she had on Flint Collins, she'd told him, and had found absolutely nothing that raised a single question mark. Other than that the man pushed the boundaries on risk-taking.

A few of his investments had seemed questionable because of the amounts and the commodities those amounts were spent on—until she'd followed them through to the sale that had grossed impressive amounts.

He'd had a few losses, too, but they were minimal in comparison.

Her father still suspected Collins was behind the thefts. However, he agreed that she should spend equal time on others in the company. She'd already started to do that.

And in the meantime, people who spent time with someone noticed things.

So maybe that was her "in" with Flint. Maybe she had to spend time with him, eyes wide open, and look for whatever could help her father.

While she simultaneously scoured the files of everyone else in the company.

If she failed, her father was going to have to go to the police. Investors would learn that Owens Investments had trouble in the ranks and the client list would dwindle.

Not only would her father's company be at risk of going under, but Flint Collins's job security would be at risk, as well—if he wasn't the thief.

So, in a way, she could be helping him by spying on him.

The thought was a stretch.

Tamara went with it anyway. She was going to help her father. She'd been her parents' only shot at being grandparents and she'd failed them there. She knew it wasn't her fault but...

She wasn't going to fail them here.

Flint had called ahead to make certain they wouldn't have to wait for a table. He'd requested a booth—strictly for the privacy. The fact that they got one by the window facing the ocean was a gift, but one he wasn't surprised to receive. He frequented the restaurant. Almost always with clients who had a lot of money to spend.

"Excuse me a second," he said, pulling out his phone as soon as they'd ordered drinks. Raspberry iced tea for both of them, something the restaurant was known for. Touching the icon for the new app he'd downloaded that morning at the Bouncing Ball Daycare, Flint waited for the portal to open. Mallory Harris had cameras installed in the nursery and with the app he could check in on Diamond Rose whenever he wanted.

Mallory was also keeping a detailed feeding spreadsheet for him—at his request—but, as it turned out, something she normally did anyway.

He'd checked in on his new family member before heading down to the lobby and his meeting with Tamara. But half an hour had passed since then.

That was the longest he'd gone without seeing his baby sister since she'd been placed in his arms the day before. In the office, he'd had his phone propped up on his desk where he could see the screen app at all times.

She'd cried twice to be fed, an hour after he'd dropped her off and then an hour and a half later. He hoped he hadn't missed the next one...

Almost as though on cue, the sound came—a little warning first, more of a cough than a cry. But if they didn't get to her soon, she'd be wailing so hard it would sound like she was going to suffocate or something.

As the second cry followed the warning, a foot hit his shin under the table.

"I'm sorry." Tamara moved in the booth, placing herself more to his left rather than directly across from him.

The accidental touching of their bodies under the table

wasn't attention-worthy. But her hands were clasped so tightly together he could see her knuckles were white.

She was tense.

Because he'd been looking at his phone rather than listening to her questions? He couldn't blame her, really; this was a business lunch. But their food hadn't even been delivered yet.

Still, he set the phone on its stand, pushing it off to his right. He could keep an eye on it and still give her his attention.

"I'm the one who should apologize," he told her in his most affable tone. "Being on my cell—that was rude of me." He couldn't afford to have her thinking that he was wasting business time on personal pursuits. He needed her to know he was in no way a threat to the company's efficiency.

On a hunch, and feeling friendly toward her due to her help the day before—the godsend her friend Mallory was turning out to be—he moved the phone so she could see.

"Mallory has cameras installed, and that means I can keep an eye on Diamond Rose," he explained. And then hastened to add, "This allows me to set my mind at ease where she's concerned so I can focus fully and completely on the job at hand. I'm all yours."

She was staring at his phone, her lips tense now, too.

"I'm glad things worked out with Mallory," she said, her delivery giving no indication that she was upset with him or his activity. On the contrary, she sounded genuine.

Diamond Rose's cries were growing more intense. Tamara looked around them and although his phone's volume was already on its lowest setting, he muted it completely. Mary Beth, the grandmotherly woman Mallory had introduced to him this morning as one of the Bouncing Ball's full-time nursery personnel, appeared on screen, scooping up the baby and holding her close.

Flint relaxed as Diamond Rose snuggled against Mary Beth. He'd made it in time for feeding.

"How'd it go last night?" Tamara was smiling at him now.

He'd thought her heaven-sent before, but that smile... Yeah, she was something.

"With the baby, I mean," she added when he failed to respond in a timely fashion. She was watching him, not his phone. And seeming to care about more than just the business reason for their lunch.

Her look felt...personal.

Of course, he *was* a bit sleep deprived.

"It was rough." He told her the truth, but he grinned, too. "Still, we made it through." He told her about the number of times the baby had cried, shortly after being fed and changed. About going back and forth between his room and hers, and his eventual desperate fix—the Pack 'n Play on the floor right next to his bed.

He was honest with her because he was done living a double life: the convict's kid and the successful businessman. Done lying to himself about who he was.

If he was going to be worthy of that completely innocent little girl taking that bottle on his screen, if he was going to teach her how to come from what they'd come from and still be a success, then he'd have to quit denying to himself that he was different from most of the people in the world he inhabited.

Not that any of this had to do with his first night with a newborn, or was in any way related to the question he'd just been asked. It was simply a reminder of the mode of thinking he was bringing into the meeting ahead. The life ahead.

Emotionally, Stella's leaving hadn't hit him as hard yet as it was bound to, but he knew he wasn't going through that again—a rejection after he was fully committed. A rejection based on something over which he had no control and couldn't change. He was the son of a convict. He'd grown up with her as the constant in his life. Loved her. And the child she'd borne on her prison deathbed. If someone was going to have a problem with the baggage he carried, at least he'd know up front. No more hiding.

He'd had enough disappointment for one lifetime.

"Obviously she didn't like being in a room alone," Tamara was saying while thoughts flew through Flint's brain at Mach speed. "She needed to be close to you, but probably not right up to the bed. I'll bet if you keep her playpen in your room, but along the wall, and put her to bed there, where she can be aware of your presence, you'll both sleep better."

He nodded, finding the concept of a baby in his room with him every night a bit...alarming, but was not completely unfond of the idea. "You seem to know a lot about children."

Her lips tensed again. But then he wasn't sure as she almost immediately smirked and said, "Mallory's my closest friend," as though that explained everything.

And he supposed it did. If Mallory shared the details of her work life on a regular basis.

"How did you two meet?" High school? Grade school, maybe? He knew plenty of people whose friendships went that far back. Whereas he didn't have any from a year ago. Or the year before that.

Other than Stella and Alana Gold, Flint had avoided personal relationships outside one-night stands.

He had clients who went almost as far back as high school, though.

"We were in a women's group together," Tamara said, glancing at his phone and then quickly away. She turned, facing the room, as though looking for their lunch.

"Businesswomen?" He wasn't going to try to explain his curiosity, but Tamara had arrived in his life at a critical time and, as a result, he felt drawn to her.

That was what he believed, anyway. "We were all women who worked, yes," she said. Then added, "Mal's one of the brightest, most successful women I know, on all levels. She's savvy and makes good money. Her day care is always close to maximum capacity, and yet she hasn't become hardened by the shadow sides of business ownership. Like the people who don't pay on time, or at all. The ones who find fault with everything. The hours. Nothing gets to her. She's a nurturer to her core."

He nodded again, not sure why she was selling her friend so hard when he'd already signed a contract with her. The deal was closed. But he liked listening to her talk. Liked how the gold rim around the green of her eyes glistened as she spoke about her friend.

Hell, he liked just sitting across the table from her.

She was there on business.

"You said you had some things to discuss with me?" He'd answer whatever questions she had and was fully confident she'd find nothing wasteful in the way he worked. Then he'd see if maybe she'd have dinner with him sometime. Just dinner. Nothing to do with business.

"Only some clarifications," she explained, taking a sip of her iced tea. Over the next twenty minutes, through the delivery of lunch and eating of same, she talked about several of his dealings during the years. Her questions were strictly from memory, no notes. She asked for justification of certain expenses, mostly making sure that she understood things as the way she thought she did.

He enjoyed talking to her about work even more than talking about her friend. He was good at what he did. One of the best around. And she was a quick and avid learner.

She also seemed genuinely interested. More than Stella had ever been.

He talked about the money saved in throwing one lavish, weekend-long yacht party for a number of investors, rather than many expensive dinners with individuals, mentioning not only the obvious savings on the event costs, but other advantages—like the adrenaline that kicked up when investors talked together about investments.

"Everyone wants to get in on the best deal," he reiterated as the waitress cleared away their plates.

"You drive the market, affect stock prices, by persuading everyone to invest in one thing," she said.

He shook his head. "We discuss the market, in small groups and as a whole, and where we think the trends are headed. Not everyone invests in the same way. They all get excited about investing in whatever they think is the best bet after all conversations are through."

She smiled as she studied him. "In other words, you drive their desire to invest," she summed up.

"Maybe. They have to *want* to invest to get involved in the conversation."

The bill was delivered and he reached for it. He'd suggested the place, but when she took it from him, he didn't try to stop her. This was her lunch, he knew it would be expensed, and he didn't want to insult her. But he hoped there'd be a next time, and that it would be his treat.

As he'd observed earlier, she'd been put in his path at a critical time. And she already knew all about his mother. She'd seen his employee file, so she'd know about his own troubles eight years before. And she'd met Diamond Rose.

She was only with him because she had to be. He didn't miss that point. But if she accepted a personal invitation...

He waited until they were almost back at the office, until they were talking about the weather, clearly not a business discussion, before he asked, "Would you be interested in doing this again sometime? Not as a date, but just having lunch together? If you come up with any more questions about what we do at Owens, I'd be happy to answer them, and you've given me so much insight on raising newborns, I'd just like to say thank you."

Anything later than lunch involved Diamond Rose, and he wasn't ready for that.

"I..." Shaking her head, she let her words trail off.

She was going to turn him down. He was more disappointed than he'd expected to be, but waited for what would no doubt be a polite brush-off.

Or, God help him, was she going to report him to Howard for sexual harassment? He hadn't touched her. Or indicated that he wanted to. He'd just invited her to lunch.

He started to sweat anyway. In his experience, based on who he was, his background, people were more apt to assume he was guilty than the guy next door. Even if he *was* the guy next door.

That mess eight years ago had nearly stolen any hope he'd had of making a decent life for himself.

His mother's death three days ago had stolen even more...

"I'd actually like that, thank you. I'm pretty sure that between now and then I'll come up with more questions and the way you explain things, enough but not too much..." Tamara said after a noticeable time had passed.

Flint had no idea why she'd changed her mind, but he was certain she had. And he was glad of it, too—enough so that he wasn't going to question his luck.

He'd press it, though. "Sometime this week?" he asked. He had a business lunch scheduled for the next day. "Thursday?"

"Thursday would be good."

Okay, then. That was set. He'd been off-line from Diamond Rose for at least twenty minutes and from commodities reports for almost two hours. Holding the door open for Tamara, he thanked her for lunch, told her to contact him if she had any other questions, then wished her a good rest of the day and hightailed it to his office.

Keeping to his priorities was paramount. That was a promise to Alana. And to Diamond Rose.

## Chapter Nine

Tamara was too busy Tuesday afternoon to think about the complexities of her lunch meeting. But they were there, a steady presence in the background of her day. She'd visited the head of every department. Had looked at their bottom lines.

Finding very little, even as an efficiency expert, to offer her father, she started to feel overwhelmed. She had some ideas on making the mail room run more smoothly. Thought maybe a delivery service would work better than the current system of having a driver on-site, ready to go if the need arose. Yes, the driver handled other menial tasks when he wasn't driving, but they were tasks that could easily be incorporated into the daily routines of several different employees.

None of which was going to make a damn bit of difference if she couldn't find something really out of place.

Granted, she'd only gone over one broker's files in

depth—Flint's. There was at least a week's worth of information to weed through, already downloaded on her computer that morning, pertaining to all accounts and monies. Everything from commissioned earnings to an annual fund-raiser to benefit underprivileged children that her father had been running around Christmastime every year since Tamara's first miscarriage.

Next, she'd be looking at supply purchases and expense reports.

And figured she could study numbers, tally up columns, run down bids and purchase orders for months and still not find what she needed.

At the end of the day, she went to her father. She needed to know more about the specifics of what his accountant had found.

"I don't think it's Flint Collins," she said the second she sat with him on the solid leather couch at the far end of his office. He'd poured her a glass of tea with ice. And had a shot of whiskey for himself.

One shot. That was what he had every day before leaving the office. His way of unwinding, he'd always said, of leaving the stresses of his business day right where they belonged.

"He's worked too hard to get where he is to jeopardize it over money," she said. That was her gut instinct. At least, that was what she called whatever it was that was driving her to want to help him.

"I went through every single client transaction, Dad. Every expense report. Granted, I didn't study every line item, or look up every purchase order, or check actual filed expense reports against his reimbursements. But I did look at a lot of them, and at overall figures. I couldn't find ten cents that had been misappropriated. Now, if he's claiming expenses he shouldn't be, that's something I can check, but I need more concrete information or I'm wasting valuable time spinning my wheels."

Naïve of her to think she'd just open up a ton of files and come across some glaring discrepancy. Or even a slightly buried one. She was used to comparing figures others didn't look at—like expenses and supplies for each person compared to others working the same or similar job. Looking for waste.

Not looking for a crime.

"I found a couple of people 'stealing' from the company I was at a couple of months ago," she continued, half afraid he was going to be disappointed in her. Which made no sense, considering her parents had been her biggest champions her entire life.

So why the feelings of guilt? As if there was something going on she didn't want him to know about?

"They worked different shifts and were taking turns clocking out for each other so they'd both get overtime pay when they weren't even working their forty-hour shifts."

"And, of course, expense reports not gelling with actual receipts and time stamps has come up more than once, since clamping down on misuse of those perks, or cutting back on some of the more extravagant ones, are the easiest ways to save a company money."

Howard sipped his whiskey. He was frowning as he studied her.

"I didn't want to prejudice you," he said when she fell silent. "And I don't want to hang Collins without giving him a fair shake," he added. "I like the guy. He's always done what he said he'd do. Every single time. Truthfully, I'm not even sure I'll press charges if it turns out to be him, as long as he makes full restitution and agrees to get out of the business permanently. Only a couple of people know about the fraud at this point. My accountant, and you. For the overall health of the business, I'd like to keep it that way."

Sitting forward, he put his glass on the table, elbows on his knees, and faced her. "Who knows? You could've found something as simple as two expense account reports coming out of one business lunch."

"Two different people claiming the same lunch?" If it was done all the time, the money would add up. She got that her father didn't want anyone in the company to know he was checking up on them, but something like that would've been easy for him to discover without her help and without raising too many alarms in his ranks.

"More like two expense reports, each claiming half of one lunch when only one employee was there."

She frowned. She could see duplicity in that but... "If they each claimed only part, then the company wouldn't be out any money."

Unless...

"You think someone, say Flint Collins, has somehow managed to secure *two* expense accounts—both in his name? And is using one to reimburse himself and the other to treat himself to a more expensive lifestyle at the company's expense?"

He supposedly had that rich girlfriend he was keeping up with, although, to date, she'd seen no indication of another woman in his life.

He'd asked her to have lunch with him. Partially, as a thank-you for helping him out with his sister. Not that she'd done anything. But would a man who was in a relationship do that?

Immediate reasons came to mind why he might. Not least of which might be that he was unethical.

"How much do you know about trading?" her father asked.

She knew there were a lot of legal guidelines; that a lot of people had used a lot of different ways to cheat while doing it. And she knew that the world's economic security revolved around the stock market.

"Not enough."

"I thought not knowing too much would make it easier for you to find what we're looking for, because obviously it's designed to be missed by those of us closely involved. I also wanted to find out if it appeared that I was doing anything shady. If you were able to discover records that put you in doubt as to my culpability. I needed to know what someone looking from the outside would find, where a trail might lead, in case it led back to me. I'm not completely sure I'm not being framed. Luckily you haven't found anything." He stood, went across the room to a row of built-in file drawers and started thumbing through folders.

She hoped that was true—that her father wasn't being framed. Because she'd held that baby and it was messing her up. She was off her game, going to fail her father, if she didn't get some help with this assignment. Maybe whatever he was looking for over there in the cabinet would make the difference, would give her a chance to deal with the way she felt and the effect it was having on her ability to do what she needed to do.

This was why Tamara didn't hold babies. Couldn't hold them.

Unlike Mallory, who'd held her son every day for almost five months before he'd died and took comfort from the feeling of a baby in her arms, Tamara had never been able to hold her own child. Not even Ryan, who'd been fully viable when he'd been born four months early.

And while, for the most part, Tamara had recovered, the one thing she could not do was hold a child. It wasn't as if a woman couldn't live a full, productive, happy life without ever holding a baby. Particularly a woman who knew she was never going to have children of her own.

Howard was back, handing her some files. "These are the basic rules of trading," he told her. "You can find the same kind of thing on the internet, but this is something I put together for a college career day I was doing a few months ago. You won't need to know any more than that."

She took the files.

He emptied his glass. "You ready to go meet your mother for dinner?" he asked. She'd taken a rain check the night before. Her mother had already cashed it in.

They stopped by her place to drop off her car and then, in the front seat of her father's Lincoln, she leafed through the material he'd given her—thinking of Flint Collins as she did.

Getting glimpses of him in his world.

Which was also her father's world, she reminded herself.

"Basically, what we're looking at here is a pattern day trader. Someone who makes a certain number of day trades over a set period of time. Four or more in five days, for example. Day traders can trade with a large enough margin to buy and sell with less in the account than is actually being spent. But a pattern day trader has real advantages in that, for him, the margin is larger. He can trade for up to four times the cash value in the account, which about doubles the normal margin. That gives him what's called 'day trader buying power' and is a measurable leverage."

She got enough of what he was saying to nod with some confidence.

"Someone in Owens Investments is using my broker license, basically signing in as me, to make trades that rose to pattern day trader status. The log-ins were from various computers in the building—any of which I could have accessed, and all in secure areas out of view of surveillance cameras. They were made at various times throughout the day.

"The trader was using monies from an account I set up for charitable donations," he explained, "without ever really withdrawing money.

"Whoever it was would make four day trades in a four-day period, meaning they bought and sold in one day, all small trades that lost nothing, but gained little, so no withdrawals were made. Then, on the fifth day, he'd use the day trader buying power to buy and sell for enormous profit."

Howard paused to take a breath as they approached the turn into the upscale neighborhood where she'd grown up.

"At the beginning and the end of every day, the account looked just as it always did, with no visible withdrawals or deposits. One of the things about pattern day trading is that accounts can't be held overnight, so there was a guarantee of ending the day the same way it began." He took another deep breath before adding, "We presume the daily profits went into an offshore account. But we've been unable to trace it due to a complicated computer trail and legalities being different from country to country."

"What happened when he—or she—made a losing trade? Was the money put back?"

"That didn't happen."

"This person traded every day without a single loss?" It meant this trader—or traitor, she thought wryly—had to be damned good.

Signaling the turn, Howard shook his head. "There were only a handful of weeks this was done. Money was made with the use of Owens Investments' funds, but there's no accounting for that cash. It looks like I made a considerable amount of money I didn't report."

Her heart was thudding in her chest. "Can you go to jail for that?"

When he shook his head a second time, Tamara almost cried with relief. "We've already submitted corrected tax returns," he said, "claiming an oversight and paying all appropriate taxes and fees."

"On money you never had."

"That's right. There's a lot more to it, of course. I'm giving you a vastly simplified version. But you've got the gist. The only other thing we found were those expense reports, splitting bills. They were always split between various brokers and me. Basically, someone was tagging me onto various expense reports, from every broker in the house, over the past year."

"Someone was turning in expense reports in your name?" she asked, incredulous.

"That's right."

"What happened with the money?"

"I have all my expense-report checks deposited directly into the charitable donation account."

They'd turned into the long circular drive, pulling up to the fountain in front of her parents' home. That fountain had been the site of family photos commemorating just about every meaningful event in her life—including each time she'd come home to tell her parents she was pregnant.

They'd taken one when she'd left to move to Boston, too. She'd been sick to her stomach that day. And felt like throwing up now, too.

"Who in the company knows you don't keep expense monies reimbursed to you? Who knows you deposit them?"

"Any number of people. My top management, of course. It's a tax write-off. I offer the option to all my managers. But others know, too."

"Which traders know?"

He shrugged but his glance was filled with sadness as he said, "Any of them could, depending on whether or not the people I've told have talked about it."

"Have you ever told any of your traders directly?"

Her stomach in knots, she knew what was coming. She knew why her father suspected Flint Collins.

"One," he said. "Because he mentioned at the Christmas Charity Fund Auction a couple of years ago that he wanted to give back to the company by way of charitable donation. So I told Flint Collins and offered to have his monies deposited into the account."

And Flint Collins, she knew, as a top producer, was inarguably good enough to have made the trades in question without a loss.

He was also a risk-taker. The day she'd met him, he'd made the company an incredible amount of money on a deal that could easily have lost a bundle.

Her heart felt as though it had been pumped full of lead.

"Did he take you up on the offer?"

"Yeah. Until he started dating Stella Wainwright. That was when he bought the Lincoln SUV. I heard of at least two weekend trips he took to exotic locations using a private jet. And he quit donating to the charitable account."

The rich girlfriend had a name.

Tamara didn't want to care anymore whether she existed or not.

She cared about her lunch date on Thursday, though. She might not be making any real progress within the company, but she had an in, just the same. A way to help her father.

She was going to get to know Flint Collins. To infiltrate his life as much as he'd let her and find out everything she could about him.

Just as a supposed friend, of course. She wasn't going

to prostitute herself. Besides, she'd already made up her mind that if by some chance the man turned out to be innocent, she still wouldn't pursue any attraction she might feel for him. But maybe she'd try to set him up with Mallory. If he was half as good a guy as he led one to believe, they'd be perfect for each other.

*If* he wasn't a crook.

Mallory and Diamond Rose would be perfect for each other. That was what she was really thinking.

As she followed her father into the house, she thought about Stella Wainwright. Wondered about her. Planned to look up her father's firm when she got home. Only for Mallory's sake. Or Diamond's.

In the event that Flint Collins was on the up-and-up.

Yeah, she was bothered about the woman—for Mallory's sake. Which meant she was getting ahead of herself.

Wait until the man's name was cleared first.

Or not cleared.

Then try to find out more about his girlfriend.

Like, why the woman wasn't helping the poor guy, leaving him to sleep with a Pack 'n Play next to his bed so he could get a few minutes' rest.

Again, not her problem.

Or concern.

So why, as she put on a bright face for her parents and focused on giving them no cause for worry on her behalf, was she still thinking about Flint Collins and how he seemed to deserve more than he was getting from Stella Wainwright?

## Chapter Ten

Flint had slept better on Tuesday night. Taking Mallory's advice, he'd laid down as soon as Diamond Rose did after dinner and then alternated dozing and lounging for the rest of the night whenever she slept. He hadn't gotten anything else done, but he'd woken on Wednesday morning feeling a hell of a lot better than he had since the call from the prison warden telling him his mother had passed away.

Wednesday evening wasn't as good. He'd set it up to be—had had a great lunch with one of his most lucrative clients and a successful afternoon of trading because of it.

And Diamond Rose seemed to be getting into a schedule of eating every two hours and sleeping well in between. He'd watched her on and off all day, and Mallory's report had been positive.

He'd even dared a stop at the grocery story on the way home from the day care, disconnecting the carrier from the car seat as if he'd been doing it all his life, looping the handle over his forearm and setting it into the grocery cart as soon as he got inside.

If he'd been on the lookout for a woman, he would've been amused by the attention he was getting from the few after-work shoppers—obviously so based on their business attire—who were, like him, he imagined, buying something for a quick dinner.

Two of them met his gaze and smiled. A third stopped and reached down, as though to pull back the blanket looped over the handle of the carrier, effectively building a tent around Diamond Rose. But his quick turn forestalled that move. The woman apologized, said she was a single mom of two little ones, then handed him her card and said to give her a call if he had any questions or needed help or advice.

How she'd known he wasn't married, he had no idea. And then, upon further reflection as he walked the aisles, he wondered if she hadn't cared one way or the other.

Which led him back to the place he'd landed, on and off, all day. Tamara Frost. She'd accepted his invitation to lunch. He'd casually mentioned her to Mallory when he'd received his personal report on Diamond Rose's day, but had gleaned nothing, other than that she worked hard and excelled at her job.

Things he already knew.

He paused at the deli, considering premade pork barbecue and coleslaw. Both looked one step away from congealed.

In his other life he'd have treated himself—and Stella— to an expensive dinner. As it was, he settled for frozen lasagna that could do what it needed to do in the oven without his supervision.

He made it home without mishap. He'd timed it so that Diamond Rose slept through the entire outing. He put his food in the oven and, when she woke up, was ready with a diaper and a warm bottle. He had her back to sleep in record time and was considering a beer—the hardest he liked his alcohol most days—when there was a knock on his door.

He wasn't expecting anyone and didn't ever have drop-in visitors. His thoughts immediately flew to the police, coming to bring yet another bout of bad news about his mother. He was halfway to the door before he realized it wouldn't be the police. At least not about his mother.

He was never going to have another of those visits. The awareness settled on him—with relief, since he was free from that dread now, and with sadness, too. His mother was gone. Any hope he'd held of her ever turning herself around was gone with her.

To his shock, a uniformed officer stood outside his door.

"Are you Flint Collins?" the woman asked.

"Yes."

"You've been served, sir," she said, handing him an envelope.

By the time he glanced from it to her, all he could see was her back.

Tense from the inside out, Flint glanced at the baby sleeping in her carrier on his kitchen table, with the idiotic idea that he didn't want to open the envelope in front of her. Whatever it was, he was going to shield her from it.

Shield her from a life in which officers appeared at your door—for any reason at all.

Was he being sued?

Or, God forbid, was someone after Diamond Rose? Challenging his right to her?

Turning around, he tore open the envelope. No one was taking the baby from him. He had money. He'd fight...

*What the hell?*

He'd been issued a restraining order. By Stella. Reading it, he could hardly believe what he was seeing. Stella was afraid he was going to hurt her. That he was going to retaliate for her breaking up with him. He was not to distribute any pictures of her that might be in his possession. He was to gather up any of her belongings still in his home—she'd provided a list—and leave them outside his front door, at which point the woman who'd delivered the order would take them and would leave a box of his things in return.

The next sheet was a legal agreement whereby he agreed not to attach to any Wainwright holdings, not to mention them, or say he'd ever been associated with them, not to claim anything of theirs as his, for any reason. Stella agreed to the same, regarding him and his family. It was further understood that any child he had in his custody had no relation to, or bearing on, her.

When he got through the last sheet, he started back at the first. She'd gone to court and requested a restraining order. There was a legal document filed with his name on it. A court date would be set within the next three weeks to allow him to dispute the claims therein, and the order would either be dropped for lack of cause or put into effect for up to three years.

It was the paragraph on the second page that got to him. *Defendant.* Him. He was a defendant. His whole life, even eight years before, he'd managed to keep himself clean, no charges filed against him ever. And now...he was a defendant?

Flint's entire being slumped with fatigue. The weight on his shoulders seemed about to push him to the floor as he read the claim.

*Defendant has a history of criminal influence and, upon victim asking to end relationship, wouldn't take*

*no for an answer to the point of victim being fright-
ened for her and her family's safety and well-being.*

When Stella had said she was breaking up with him,
he'd given her a chance to calm down, to get used to the
idea of the secret he'd kept about his mother's identity. Because Stella had known the man he'd become. Collins was
a common enough name. There'd been no reason for her
to remember a court case from eight years before when
it had had nothing whatsoever to do with her area of law.
Small-time drug dealers didn't touch corporate lawyers.

But she'd looked up the case. And when, after a few
hours, he'd stopped by her office to see her, thinking they
could talk, she'd been pissed off. He'd waited outside and
she'd warned him not to stalk her.

*Stalk her?*

That had been that. He'd left. And hadn't tried to contact her since.

He was no threat. Had never been a threat.

But the Wainwright name was apparently too pristine
to be linked, in any way, with his.

Or Diamond Rose's.

In the end, that was what stuck in his throat. The fact
that she'd mentioned his newborn baby in her dirty court
papers.

Glancing at the sleeping baby, he grabbed a garbage bag,
collected the things on Stella's list, down to the toothbrush
he'd meant to throw away, thankful he'd been too distracted
to do that yet—could he be sued for a toothbrush?—and
left the bag out on the porch, looking over at the waiting
unmarked car at his curb. He'd sign her document in the
morning, with a notary present.

And he'd call an attorney, too. One who was good
enough at his or her job to go head-to-head with the Wainwrights. He wanted the whole mess gone before anyone

was the wiser. Wanted no evidence it had ever existed. There was no way in hell he was going to live under the threat of a restraining order for the next three years. Anytime Stella wanted to, she could "run into" him somewhere and claim he'd violated the order. He could end up in jail.

The idea gave him the cold sweats. His whole life, everything he'd worked for...

He was going to "be someone," his mother had told him so many times. What he'd taken her words to mean was that he'd never see the inside of a jail cell.

He'd barely escaped the nightmare eight years before. And had been hell-bent ever since on making sure he never came remotely close again.

He wasn't a defendant. Wasn't ever going to be a defendant. That order had to go away.

When the baby awoke, he was bothered enough by Stella's bombshell that he forgot to be nervous about giving his little one her first bath. Mallory had offered him some pointers and he'd watched several internet videos, too.

He talked to Diamond Rose the whole time, taking care to keep his voice soft, reassuring. He'd turned up the heat in the house first, kept the water tepid and a towel close so she wouldn't get cold, and he worked as rapidly as he could with big hands on such a small, slippery body. In the end, the two of them got through the process without any major upsets.

Something else came out of the evening. Any feelings he might still have had for Stella were washed down the drain with the dirty bathwater.

Too bad about his frozen dinner, though. It dried out in the oven.

Tamara had expected Flint to take her to an establishment not unlike the one they'd visited for lunch on Tuesday.

Instead they'd gone to Balboa Park, sitting in the sun on a cement bench, having a wrap from a nearby food truck—possibly one of the best-tasting meals she'd ever had.

With a man she found more attractive than any other man she'd ever shared lunch with. Business or otherwise.

What was it about Flint Collins that did this to her? It wasn't like he was drop-dead model material, not that she went for that type. Yeah, he was fine-looking—enough that she'd noticed several other women checking him out during the time they'd been in the park. But the blond hair and brown eyes, the more than six-foot-tall lean frame, even the expensive clothes, could've been matched by any number of other "California blond" men. The state was flooded with them.

"I saw a brochure at the Bouncing Ball this morning," he told her. "The founder of this food truck is a lawyer in Mission Viejo and a former client of Mallory's."

"You're talking about Angel's food truck! I didn't know it had been renamed!" she said, glad to have something other than his sexuality to think about. It's a Wrap fit the menu better. It wasn't fancy, but she liked it so much more. It was as though he'd known she'd prefer sitting in the park during her lunch hour to being trapped at a table in a fancy restaurant. She spent a lot of the day trapped in a seat at a desk.

"I never met the couple because I was in Boston," she continued, "but Mallory called me about the case from the first day she met them. The woman wanted Mal's help in identifying her abducted son, without alerting his father, the abductor, to the fact that he'd been found out."

"Why not just call the police?"

"Not enough evidence for them to do anything. The woman was acting on instinct, based on a picture she'd seen at the day care."

"What did Mallory do?"

"She helped her! Without giving up any confidential information, or putting the child or his father at risk, in case the man wasn't guilty. Anyway, it all turned out well."

He was staring at her as though he couldn't get enough. Of her story, she had to remind herself, not of her.

"So...it was the woman's son?"

"Yeah. And Mal was the one who got the proof."

Flint Collins's full attention was a heady thing. Wiping everything else from her mind. And—

This wasn't going to help her father.

He'd pulled out his phone. Had it on his thigh. She couldn't hear any sounds coming from it, but realized, if she glanced at the screen, she'd see the newborn child he'd taken on that week.

Busy avoiding that choice, she wanted to ask if he knew anything about offshore accounts, but couldn't figure out a legitimate reason for wanting to know.

And wondered why he'd asked her out to lunch.

"How's everything going at home?" she asked instead. Not a Stella question. Unless he happened to mention her in the course of his answer.

He told her about Diamond Rose's first bath, complete with turning up the heat in the house. And her heart gave another little flip.

Because of the baby, she told herself.

What kind of fate was forcing her to spend time with a man who had an infant? And be attracted to him to...

"I've been trying to work up to asking if you'd like to join us for an evening," he said as they finished their wraps and threw away the trash, walking side by side as they made their way through the park to where they'd catch a cab back to the office. They'd spent all of twenty minutes together.

"Us?" she asked, concentrating on her step, keeping it steady. She had to do this. To pretend to be friends with him. And it wasn't like she freaked out anytime she was around an infant. She flew on planes with them. Ate in restaurants with them. She just kept her distance.

"Diamond Rose and me." He'd put his phone in his shirt pocket, his hands in the pockets of his dress pants.

She suddenly felt hot and waited for the chill that would sweep over her when the flash ended.

Maybe she really was getting the flu.

Could she at least hope so?

"I'd like that," she told him while hoping the thrill she felt was because she was one step closer to helping her father.

For the next couple of steps she warred with herself over whether or not she should say more—perhaps tell him she had baby issues.

But she didn't tell anyone that except the people to whom she was closest.

Besides, this wasn't a real friendship.

"When?" she asked as their arms touched.

"Tomorrow night? I can make lasagna tonight so we'd just have to heat it up. We could watch a movie."

What about Stella? She had to ask.

"I might be out of line here, but…are you seeing anyone? I…like to know what I'm walking into." No. Wrong. All wrong.

Now it sounded as if she was interested in starting a "seeing each other" relationship. Which she wasn't. She couldn't.

Could she?

In any case, she'd had no business asking.

"Not anymore I'm not," he said. "I was until recently."

"How recently?"

"Last week."

Oh. So, she was…some kind of rebound?

Strangely, that felt okay. Was actually growing on her. A friendship—maybe even a real one?—while he adjusted his life. Because even if he turned out to be her father's thief, Howard wasn't planning to press charges. Yes. This could all work. She could help her father, and maybe be friends for real. Someday. When this was all over.

They just had to make sure those erroneous trades never occurred again.

"Stella wasn't ready to take on a child," Flint said into the silence that had fallen, as though he thought she'd been waiting for more explanation.

She didn't mind knowing what had happened.

"She might come around," she offered, feeling inane.

He shook his head, his hair glinting like gold in the midday sun.

Another few weeks and the park would be decorated for Christmas.

What if their friendship was real? *Became* real? Would they still be friends by Christmastime?

If so, they could bring the baby down here to see the lights.

Her step faltered. If she kept her distance from the child—no physical contact—she'd probably be okay. Knowing from the outset that the friendship was, at most, only temporary.

And even if she wasn't okay, she'd do what had to be done. For her father. Her parents. She was all they had. Or ever would have, as far as blood family went.

"She gave me an ultimatum," he said after waiting for a crowd of schoolchildren to cross their path. "The baby or her."

She knew which he'd chosen. And felt she had to say something.

"Some women just aren't meant to be mothers." Wow. Hadn't meant for her own mantra to slip out.

But maybe it was best that he know, going in, that there could never be more than friendship between them. That she, like Stella, wasn't meant to be a mother.

Even if he turned out not to be guilty, even if they developed a genuine friendship, she was planning to set him up with Mallory. Mallory was perfectly suited to be everything he and Diamond Rose could ever want.

"She wants children," he said. "Just not the bastard child of an incarcerated convict."

The way he said the words—she looked at him—was he the one Stella hadn't wanted? The bastard child of a convict? Or had it really been because he'd wanted to bring his sister into their family?

"You don't sound all that bitter about it." Which surprised her. He had every right to be.

"I'm not. I'm thankful I discovered her lack of mutual respect before we got married and had children, rather than afterward. And to be fair to her, I'd failed to tell her that my mother was in prison."

They'd reached the curb.

He hailed a cab.

## Chapter Eleven

By Friday afternoon Flint was feeling pretty good about himself. He'd met with Michael Armstrong, an attorney who'd come highly recommended by one of the clients who'd been with him the longest.

They could be as little as a phone call away from having the order dropped. Michael was certain he could negotiate a mutual agreement between him and the Wainwrights that would prevent either party from bad-mouthing the other, and that he could do it without a court order. Flint was willing to sign anything to that effect as long as they dropped the order.

Otherwise he was going to fight it. He had to. For Diamond Rose's sake. To let it stand unanswered meant it would be put into full effect. It would make him look guilty.

Michael was fairly confident, as was Flint, that the Wainwrights wouldn't want the matter to go to court.

While Flint was comfortable enough with the situation still open, after talking to Michael he felt one hell of a lot better going into the weekend.

The lasagna was already in the oven and Diamond Rose fed and asleep when Tamara pulled into his drive. He'd offered to send a cab for her. She'd preferred her own transportation.

He was pleased with the fact that she'd agreed to come to his house at all. She knew about his past. And had accepted his invitation anyway.

"Wow, this place is nice," she said as he opened the front door into a large entryway with a step-down living room to one side and a great room on the other. It had a wall of windows that opened up to a tiled patio and swimming pool beyond. The outdoor lighting was on and showed the pool, with the waterfall, at its best. He couldn't afford to be right on the ocean, but the pool had been a nice compromise. She turned toward the great room.

"I've got someone coming to put a wrought-iron gate around the pool," he said as he followed her through the room he'd furnished with a complete home theater arrangement, including big leather furniture with charging plug-ins. Stella had thought the room too big for intimate conversation. Too "masculine."

Diamond Rose, in her Pack 'n Play on the floor in the living room, was out of sight, but her monitor rested securely in the back pocket of his jeans.

He stood back as Tamara moved through an archway into the kitchen, which ran almost half the length of the house. One end held an informal eating area with bay windows and the other housed a more formal dining room set. A set his mother would have loved and had never seen.

He'd purchased the high-top suite for eight soon after meeting Stella.

"Dinner smells wonderful," she said, stopping to look at the pool out the kitchen window.

He wanted to tell her she *looked* wonderful. In leggings and a white shirt, gathered at the waist in back, that fell just past the tops of her thighs, with her amber hair loose and falling around her shoulders... He was sure he'd never seen anyone so beautiful.

And was getting way ahead of himself.

She'd turned. Was leaning against the counter, the window at her back with the landscape lighting a soft glow around her.

Maybe he'd pushed things too far, too fast. Having her over for dinner. It wasn't his normal approach.

But nothing about his life was normal anymore.

Nor was anything about this woman. The way she'd showed up in his life at the exact moment she had, preventing him from being fired long enough for him to make the trade that had, he was certain, ensured him his job. And then, when he'd been frantic about Diamond Rose, finding it impossible to calm her, in walked Tamara, who'd calmed her almost instantly.

He might not believe in karma and all the woo-woo stuff his mother used to spout, but he couldn't resist wondering, once again, if Alana Gold, in her death, was sending him her own version of karma. Proving that good was rewarded. That there was help beyond self-reliance.

That miracles really could happen...

"I, um, have to talk to you."

Little good ever came of those words.

He'd been about to get a bottle of wine. Stopped before he'd actually opened the refrigerator door.

His weekend took a nosedive. "What's up?"

"You told me about your ex and...I need to tell you something."

"You know Stella?" It was the first thought that sprang to mind. Was his ex-fiancée having him watched? He wouldn't put it past her. She was going to hang him out to dry for deceiving her by not telling her he wasn't from a nice, clean, *rich* family like hers. For daring to think she'd be willing to raise his dirty mother's orphaned child.

"No!" Tamara frowned, cocking her head to look at him. "Of course not. I just…need to be honest with you about something."

"Wine first," he said, grabbing the bottle of California Chardonnay. He opened it and poured two glasses, handing one to her without asking if she wanted it.

She took a sip, nodded.

Taking that as a win, he scooped up the platter of grapes and cheese he'd prepared and carried it into the dining area. Pulling out one of the chairs for her before seating himself perpendicular to her—where he could also glance across the L-shaped entryway and into the living room.

Tamara had said she needed to be honest with him. He had to listen.

And hope that whatever she had to say wouldn't be as bad as he was imagining. It would be a shame to have a second lasagna dinner drying out in the oven that week. Especially since he'd spent an hour the night before talking to a sleeping Diamond Rose while he'd prepared it.

"I—" Tamara looked at him, her expression…odd. He couldn't figure out why.

Glancing away, she took a grape, put it in her mouth, and he had an instant vision of a movie he'd seen once at a bachelor party. Tamara had a way of making a grape look even sexier than that, and she was fully dressed.

"I don't normally… I haven't ever…talked about this with anyone but my closest friends, so bear with me here."

He wanted to let her off the hook, to tell her that honesty was overrated. But after the week he'd had, the life he'd had, he couldn't do it.

No more stabs in the back, bonks over the head or officers at his door. He had Diamond Rose to protect.

He considered telling her that whatever she was struggling to say could wait. After all, they were just getting to know each other.

But he sensed that they weren't. She'd been more than a casual business introduction since the second she'd walked into Bill Coniff's office at the beginning of the week. Clearly she'd sensed something, too, or she wouldn't be about to share a confidence that only those closest to her had the privilege of knowing.

"I'm not ever going to have children." For all her struggle, she almost blurted out the words.

Did she somehow think he wanted her to? He then remembered the day before, when he'd told her that Stella had said it was either the baby or him.

"That's not really how I meant it to come out." She smiled but her lips were trembling. Flint had to consciously resist an urge to take her hand in his. To have some sort of contact between them.

"Before your... Before she wakes up—and before... Well, so you know going in... I can't do babies." Her face reddened and she was clasping her hands again, the way she'd done that day in his office.

"You were great with her," he said, assuming she needed reassurance for some reason. "The moment you picked he up, she stopped crying."

She shook her head, pushed her wineglass farther away. He had yet to take a second sip from his.

"You don't understand."

He was pretty sure of that.

"I—I can't have children."

"Okay. It's not a problem, Tamara. You figure I'm going to think less of you or something? We all have our crosses to bear." Thinking he sounded like an idiot, he continued. "I mean, I'm sorry for you, if it was something you wanted. I don't mean to trivialize that, but…"

Pulling her wineglass toward her, she took another sip. Her glass shook as she raised it to her lips and he just wanted to do whatever it took to put her at ease.

"I don't know what to say," he murmured.

She nodded. "No one does. Look, I wouldn't have brought it up, but…I've been through some…hard times. Not that I need to unload all of that on you when you've been nice enough to make me homemade lasagna, which I love. But the end result is…I keep my distance from babies. And I don't hold them. Ever."

But she had. Just three days ago.

He remembered her odd behavior then. The way she'd clasped her hands so tightly. Wringing them. Had gone for the door. And when she'd turned back, hadn't looked at Diamond Rose again. She'd been in some deep emotional pain and had done a remarkable job of covering it.

"In Bill's office, when the monitor went off, you heard that cry…" He let his words fade away, wishing he could do something to ease her pain.

She nodded. Took a piece of cheese. Bit off a small corner and played with the rest.

"Can you tell me what happened?"

With the cheese between the fingers of both hands, she shook her head, then let go with one hand to grab her wineglass. "You don't have to do this."

For some reason he did. Covering her cheese hand with his own, Flint said, "I want you to tell me."

How could he get to know her better without finding out? How could he help her if he didn't know?

How else could he understand?

Because, God knew, he wasn't just going to walk away. She'd been sent into that office on Monday for a reason.

She seemed to be weighing the decision. As though fighting a battle. Whether or not to trust him?

Then she glanced up and met his gaze. He felt like he'd won.

"I've been pregnant four times."

Flint's jaw dropped. Whatever he'd been expecting, it hadn't been that. She didn't wear a ring and had asked if he was involved with anyone. He hadn't even thought to ask if she was. He'd been a little preoccupied.

He wasn't generally a person who only considered himself. Alana Gold had taught him that through her own bad example.

He didn't regret asking Tamara to confide in him, but he was ill-prepared.

Questions bounced through his mind. All he came out with was, "What happened?"

"I lost them all."

Four small words. So stark. And carrying such an incredible depth of pain. He admired her for being able to sit there relatively composed.

He'd asked for this. He owed it to her to see it through. "Why?"

Her smirk, and accompanying shrug, held grief he was pretty sure he couldn't even begin to imagine.

"There was no obvious explanation," she said. "My husband and I both went through a battery of tests. Sometimes genetics aren't compatible. There're myriad physical causes. But nothing showed up. Which was why they said there was no reason we shouldn't keep trying."

So many questions. Things he wanted to ask. But this wasn't the time.

What did she need him to know?

"And you tried four times."

She nodded. Took a sip of wine. "Yep." She was staring at her glass and he wondered what she saw there. Wished there was some way he could take on some of her pain, help her deal with it.

Alana Gold had taught him well on that count, too. When he'd been able to keep her happy, she'd stayed clean. It was when she'd needed things he couldn't provide that they'd lost everything.

Tamara Frost had helped him. He felt deeply compelled to help her in return.

"Then what?"

Her gaze shot to his. "What do you mean, then what?"

He squeezed her hand, let it go. "Did they eventually discover a reason for what was happening? What was going wrong?"

She shook her head. "No." And when she looked at him again, there was a mixture of determination and vulnerability in her glistening eyes. "I couldn't do it anymore," she said. "I don't even want to be pregnant. I can't bear the thought of all those weeks of fear and hope, the unknown, not being in control. My own frenetic state of mind would create issues even if the fetus was healthy…"

"And your husband?" It seemed the appropriate time to ask that one.

"We're divorced, by mutual agreement. By the time we lost Ryan, we'd already drifted so far apart…"

"Ryan?" She'd named each lost fetus?

"He was viable," she said as though that explained everything. It didn't.

"I don't—"

"The others… I lost them at six, nine and eleven weeks. Still within the first trimester. But Ryan… He made it far enough to have a chance of survival. I could feel him moving inside me. I was showing. And I was sure that with him—"

She'd lost her last hope with the loss of her fourth child. Understanding came softly, but clearly. Because she was talking to someone who knew exactly when he'd lost his last hope.

Eight years before, when his mother had used the home he'd bought her to run a drug lab, implicating him in her criminal acts.

After that he couldn't help Alana anymore. Couldn't have anything to do with a future that involved her being out of prison and the two of them together. He'd visited her, because he loved her. Because she'd given him life. But he'd kept an emotional distance that had been necessary for his own mental health.

"There comes a time when you have to let go," he said aloud. Whatever the cause of the emotional pain, there came a time when you knew you'd reached the end of your ability to cope. You had to turn away. Say *no more.* "Ryan was your time."

Her gaze locked with his, those green eyes large, their gold rims more pronounced. "You get it."

He did.

And while he had no idea where it left them, with Diamond Rose sleeping in the next room, he knew for certain that their meeting had been no mistake.

She'd helped him.

He was supposed to help her.

## Chapter Twelve

The baby cried.

Tamara sipped her wine, telling herself that whatever spell had bound her and Flint Collins had been broken.

He was still watching her.

"You need to go get her," she said.

He nodded. "She has to be changed and then fed," he agreed. "It'll take me about twenty minutes. You want to set the table in the meantime? The lasagna is due to come out in about thirty."

Could she do this? A flash of her father's worried face assured her she could.

"I can do that," she told him. She'd see if he had lettuce. She could make a salad. Salad went well with Italian food. And wine.

She had another sip.

Focus. That was all it took.

That and topping off the glass of wine Flint had poured

for her. Two was her limit. Or she'd have to hang around an extra hour before she drove. She found dishes. Set the kitchen table because of the gorgeous view of the pool from the bay windows.

No. Because there'd be no view at all of the baby sleeping in the living room.

She hadn't known that was where the playpen was until Diamond Rose started to cry. Then she'd had to fight to avoid looking at the room.

But...Flint needed to see the child. For his own sake and the baby's.

Gathering up the dishes and silverware, Tamara moved them to the dining room, placing them so he could see the living room and her back was to it.

Yes, that worked fine.

And she made salad. Cutting the carrots, peeling a cucumber, chopping onion, tearing lettuce. She did it all with precise focus. When Flint's voice broke through her concentration, soft and from a distance, she chopped with more force. The newborn cried once. Tamara replayed in her head the conversation she'd had with her father the day before.

Diamond Rose was a precious little baby who had nothing to do with her. Tamara wanted the best for her. Hoped to God that everything worked out so Flint could continue to care for his sister. If that was what was best.

And it seemed to be.

Flint was different from any other man she'd ever met. He had an emotional awareness she'd never seen in a male before—yet he was masculine and sexy and exuded strength at the same time.

In one conversation, and a sketchy one at best, he'd understood more about her emotional struggle than Steve had in all their years of marriage.

For the first time since she'd lost Ryan, she felt understood.

By a man who might be a thief.

And since her father wasn't planning to press charges, because of the hit his reputation— and then the company— would take if investors knew he'd been frauded, Flint should be free to raise Diamond Rose.

"She's back to sleep."

A piece of lettuce flew out of her hand and onto the floor when she heard his voice behind her. Focus could do that to a girl—take her right out of her surroundings.

"That's impressive." He was smiling as he pointed to her neat piles of chopped vegetables.

"You make your own dressing?" She'd found four jars, with varying labels, lined up in the door of the refrigerator. She'd chosen the creamy Italian to mix in before serving their salads.

"I've been putting meals together pretty much since I could walk, it seems," he said. "By the time I was about eight, I couldn't stand the sight of peanut butter sandwiches anymore, so I asked my mom to teach me to cook."

"She was a good cook?"

"Yes, she was."

There was hesitation in his tone. And she wondered if there was more to the story. Like, when she was sober she was a good cook. Or, when she wasn't in jail she was a good cook. Tamara didn't know many of the details of his growing up, but she knew enough to fill in some of the blanks with at least a modicum of accuracy.

Within minutes they had dinner on the table and were sitting down to eat. He didn't mention the baby at all. She didn't ask, either. But it felt…unfair, somehow, doing that to him. Making him keep such a momentous change in his life all to himself.

A friend wouldn't do that. And posing or not, she had to be a good friend if she was going to find out more about him.

"It doesn't send me into a tailspin to hear about babies," she told him, spearing a bit of salad on her fork. "You can talk about her."

"I just want to make sure I know the boundaries first," he said. "I need to know what you can and can't handle."

"What I can't do is hold her." The words jumped out. "That's my trigger. The rest, I can manage. I can close my eyes if it starts to get me. Or walk away."

There. She relaxed a bit.

"But the other day…you picked her up so naturally."

"And I've been paying for it ever since." Wow…she was playing her part better than she'd ever suspected she could. She was being more honest with him than she was with anyone, including her parents.

Maybe because she knew he wouldn't be in her life all that long? Or because he was an outsider who wouldn't be hurt by her pain?

Maybe because she wasn't *completely* playing a part?

"Paying for it how?" he asked between bites of his salad.

"The first night I think I was up more than you were." And, based on what he'd later told her about it, that was saying a lot. "I have nightmares. And panic attacks."

She was tempted to say she had hot and then cold flashes, since she was having another series right now. But she'd had the first one before she'd known about Diamond Rose.

Speaking of which…

"Did you name her? Diamond Rose—it's such an unusual name."

"No." He finished his salad. "My mother did."

As he started in on his lasagna, he told her about the

names Gold, Flint, Diamond—and the rose. Expensive, beautiful, sweet.

*And fragile*, she added silently.

She'd taken her first bite of lasagna and was too busy savoring the taste to talk. She loved to cook. Considered herself good at it. He was better.

"It was the first time," she said out of the blue. She'd just swallowed that bite. Wanted to think about the second. Another sip of wine. Or the way Flint's shoulders filled out the black polo shirt he was wearing with his jeans. But she wasn't. She was still thinking about that baby.

"The first time you'd held a baby?" Leave it to him to catch right on. Did the man never miss a beat?

She nodded.

"In how long?"

"Since I lost Ryan, if you don't count the few times we tried in my therapy sessions, which I don't count because I never managed to hold the infant by myself."

Fork hovering over his lasagna, he paused before skewering another bite. "How long has it been?"

"Three years." Hard to believe it had been that long. That brought on another surge of panic. Her life was passing by so quickly.

"And how long since your divorce?"

"Two and a half years. He's remarried." And could be expecting a child any day or week or month.

"Are you two on friendly terms?"

"We talk." She didn't consider Steve a friend. He'd robbed her of her one chance to hold her son, having the baby swept away the second he'd been delivered, and asking the doctor to give Tamara something to calm her down, which had knocked her out. But their split had been amicable. Mutual. They remained…acquaintances.

She drank a little more of her wine. Had to wait a minute before sending anything more solid down her throat. Floundering, losing focus, she stared at her plate. Reminded herself what she was doing here.

"What about you and Stella? You think you'll remain friends?"

She heard the stupidity of that question even as she asked it—since the woman had ditched him because he was taking in his mother's child to raise. But desperation drove many things. Including stupid questions to fill the silence.

"I have no desire to. So, no."

Okay, then. That was clear.

But her father had said that Flint's spending habits had changed when the rich girlfriend came into his life. She had to get around to that somehow.

Or segue into offshore accounts.

She was drawing a blank.

Because she wasn't focused.

Maybe over dessert.


He knew how he could help her. Not the details, not yet. But Flint had a goal now. Find a way to repay Tamara, or the fates, for helping him out on one of the worst days of his life.

Not quite the worst. Because in another way, it might have been the absolute best. He wasn't alone anymore. He had a sister. A brand-new human being to raise.

He had family.

And it now seemed obvious to him that his payback was in helping Tamara heal enough to have a family of her own, too. To someday have a baby of her own to raise. There were other options if she couldn't give birth herself.

His and Diamond Rose's payback, really. They both owed her.

That infant sister of his already had a job to do. Because that was what you did when you planned to amount to something in life. You used the gifts you were given. You worked as hard as you could. You helped others.

The things he'd taught himself somehow. Or a message given to him subliminally in his crib.

His little sister's talents might not be clear yet, but for now, being an infant was all it was going to take.

The connection seemed unmistakable to him. Diamond Rose, who'd been screaming her lungs out, had instantly calmed when Tamara had picked her up.

Sign one.

Sign two. Tamara, who hadn't held a baby in years, who considered herself unable to hold one, had picked up Diamond Rose.

Still piecing things together, he had no idea how it was all going to work. What he should or shouldn't do. But he felt confident, as Tamara helped him with the dishes, that the answers would come to him.

He had the basics down anyway.

"I should be going," she said as soon as the dishes were done and the counters wiped. He'd put some of the leftover lasagna in a container for her. One serving was all she'd take, suggesting he put the rest in serving-size portions in the freezer, so that on nights when the baby wasn't co-operating, he could still eat a good dinner.

He'd been freezing portions for years, but didn't tell her that. He was too busy enjoying the fact that she was looking out for him, too. Stella had been mostly about what he could do for her, and he'd been all right with that. Even comfortable with it. And usually insisted on it.

"You want to do this again? Sunday maybe?" He felt confident asking. Some things you just knew.

"What time?"

"You name it. I'll be working at home all day."

She preferred afternoon to evening. He was fine with that, too.

Following her to the door, he moved closer, intending to kiss her good-night. Her expression stopped him before he'd made his intention obvious. She was worried about getting out the door without seeing the baby, not thinking about kisses.

He watched her walk to her car and only after she'd pulled out of his driveway and was out of sight did he close the door.

He really would've liked that kiss. To know her taste on his lips…

Probably just as well, though. He needed to get settled back into his career at Owens Investments and to learn how to be a dad before he took on any other committed relationship.

Friends was nice, though. Friends who helped each other…

## Chapter Thirteen

Funny how things worked themselves out. Tamara hadn't had a chance to learn anything on Friday night that could benefit her father. Then, on Saturday, while having lunch with the office manager at Owens Investments—a woman ten years older than her whom she'd never met before the previous week, but instinctively liked—the way in was handed to her.

Maria had been telling her about the system they used to keep up with the fast pace their traders required of them, and in so doing had explained quite a bit more than her father had done about his business. Maria had given her a pretty clear glimpse into the life of a stockbroker. As her father had said, the risks were great, mostly because laws were commonly broken, although it could be hard to prove. Insider trading being one of the most difficult.

She'd asked if Tamara had seen a movie from the late '80s called *Wall Street*. She hadn't. Maria had highly recommended that she watch it.

That night she found it on her streaming app and on Sunday showed up at Flint's door in black-and-white leggings, a comfy oversize white top and zebra-striped flip-flops, with the movie rented and ready. All they had to do was type her account information into his smart TV and they'd be set.

"You've never seen *Wall Street*?" he asked as he brought glasses of iced tea and a bag of microwaved popcorn for them to share.

"No. It was out before I was born," she told him. And then thought to ask, "Have you?"

Of course he would have. He was a stockbroker. And Flint seemed to study everything about anything that involved him. Like the baby, for instance. Yeah, there'd been a couple of common sense things he'd missed during his research before he'd brought his baby home, but in just those three days, he'd become better prepared than most expectant parents she'd known.

"Only about a dozen times," he told her, taking a seat on the opposite end of the couch.

Relieved that he wasn't closer, that she wasn't going to have to let him know they were "just friends," she turned to smile at him, suddenly catching sight of the Pack 'n Play in the sunken living room behind them.

Suspecting that the portable bed was there because Tamara was where she was—in the living room—she felt a crushing weight come down on her. Disappointment, yes, but far more.

A baby was being ostracized because of her.

No, that wasn't quite true. A lot of parents kept their young children separate from the family's activities while the child slept. That was why there were nurseries.

But it wasn't what she would've done if she'd had a child. It wasn't what she'd planned to do.

"Do you keep her in there when you're in here watching TV at night?"

"I'm not usually in here watching TV. I spend any free time I have on the computer. Checking stocks. My job is pretty much a 24/7 affair when I don't specifically schedule time for other things."

Like watching an old movie with her?

He'd turned on the TV. Clicked on the streaming app.

"Where's your computer?"

He nodded toward a hallway off the great-room side of the kitchen. "Down there."

"And does she stay in the living room when you're 'down there'?" She mimicked him with a grin.

No response, which she'd expected. The question had been rhetorical. Of course he didn't keep his baby in other rooms when he was there alone.

With a fancy remote that had a small phone-size keyboard on the back, he was searching for the movie. On his account.

Stood to reason that he already owned it and she'd wasted the three dollars she'd spent. Oh, well.

"You can bring her in here, Flint." She wasn't going to be the cause of any child being on the outside of any gathering ever. "I'm not so fragile that I can't be in the same room as a baby. I fly on a regular basis, and you don't get to choose who you're seated by on a plane. I'll be fine."

She wasn't convinced she would be. But at least she knew how to keep up appearances. As long as she didn't pay attention to the baby, didn't let Diamond's presence pull at her. As long as she didn't even think about picking her up.

Or doing any nurturing in a hands-on way.

"If you're sure, I'll bring her in. But only if you're completely sure that's what you want. It's not like she's going to know the difference. She's out for at least another hour."

"Like she didn't know the difference the night you tried to get her to sleep in the nursery?"

"She's used to me now. We're doing much better." His grin did things to her in inappropriate places. Probably because she was so tense about getting information for her father. And being around a newborn.

She was challenging herself personally and professionally. So it made sense that her emotions would be off-kilter.

And she might've been fighting off a flu bug the previous week, too. Her system could be in recuperation mode. Busy rebuilding antibodies.

That thought was total bunk and she knew it. She didn't have the flu. Hadn't had it the week before, either. The man was attractive. She noticed. Not a big deal.

"I want you to go get her, please," she said as he cued up the movie. "Please."

She wouldn't be able to focus on her real reason for being there if she was busy feeling bad about being the reason that baby was in the other room all alone. She was a grown woman who could take accountability for her issues, her problems. Diamond Rose was a helpless newborn who had to rely on everyone around her to fill every single one of her needs.

Besides, Tamara needed Flint relaxed if she hoped to get information that could help her father one way or the other. She'd spent most of Saturday going through files and meeting with employees who'd come in on their own time to see her, in addition to the hours with Maria in and out of the office. Her father had told her someone was trading on various computers. He knew which ones, so now she did, too. She'd wanted to find out when they were in use most often, as part of her efficiency check, so she could give her father an idea of when or why they might have been freed up for other uses. She had dates now. Other specifics.

And she was slowly making her way through expense reports and comparing them to the provided receipts, examining dates, times, employee credit card numbers, clients. Looking for…anything in the past year. Flint's records had come first. She'd finished them very late Friday night.

He'd had a lot of fancy dinners, gone to shows, on cruises, to games, with a lot of important and wealthy people. And every single dime he'd claimed checked out to the penny.

She'd told herself not to let hope grow. She'd learned the hard way that hoping led to greater heartache. Still, she'd wished she could call and tell her father that things were looking good. So far.

But, of course, she couldn't.

Just when Tamara was hooked to the point of forgetting almost everything else, a little cough jarred her. Then a tiny wail, followed by another.

She looked at Flint, who was already headed over to the playpen. "She's got another hour and a half," he said as though babies watched the clock and knew they were supposed to be hungry at certain times. Focusing on the movie, which he'd paused on the screen—about the young man learning the Wall Street ropes from someone who was at the top of his game, but had gotten there by unethical means—she waited.

"What's the matter, Little One?" Flint crooned softly. The wails grew louder. He rubbed her arm. Felt her cheek. Continued to talk. Tried to get her to take a pacifier. She continued to cry.

*Pick her up. Pick her up.*

After a few more tries with the pacifier, he picked her up.

The crying didn't stop.

For another ten minutes.

He walked with her. Talked to her about her eating schedule, explaining that it wasn't time yet. He changed her, which only made her angrier.

He left the room, taking her somewhere in another part of the house. Probably to give Tamara space. She could still hear the crying.

She couldn't just sit there, doing nothing. Poor Flint had to be getting tense. Frustrated. Especially with her there. Maybe she should leave and watch the movie another day. It wasn't as if her father had to have his answers within the next few hours.

Or that she was going to find them there that day.

The crying went on. She paced the room. Looking at bookshelves. Reading titles of DVDs. Noticing the lack of any family photos. Or personal mementoes.

Diamond Rose finally stopped crying and Tamara's entire torso seemed to settle. Until then she hadn't realized that her breathing was becoming shallow, the way it did at the onset of a panic attack. Hadn't felt herself tense.

And almost immediately the crying started again. She grabbed her purse. Had her keys and was at the door before she remembered she had to tell Flint she'd take a rain check on the movie. She couldn't just him let come out and find her gone.

Following the sounds of the baby in distress, she traveled a hallway he hadn't showed her yet, passing two rooms—a bathroom, the master suite—and eventually found him in a small back bedroom with a Jack and Jill bathroom leading into one of the rooms she'd passed.

Opening her mouth to tell him she was leaving, she

caught sight of his face. He looked scared. Honest-to-goodness scared.

"I'm sorry," he told her. "Nothing's working. She doesn't feel feverish, but maybe I should take her in."

His gaze moving from the purse on her shoulder to the keys in her hand, he nodded. "I'm sorry," he said, giving her a smile that seemed all for her, in spite of his crying infant, and went back to trying to comfort the child in his arms.

"Put her up on your shoulder," she said. "Pat her back. She might have gas."

He tried. It didn't work.

Tamara felt like crying herself. "Try rubbing her back."

That didn't work, either. Tamara had to get out of there. But she couldn't just leave him. His problems weren't hers, but he was trying so hard and she couldn't simply walk out.

"Do you have a rocking chair?"

He nodded, left the room, and she followed him. Into another room filled with baby furniture and paraphernalia. There was a mobile over the crib, but nothing on the walls. No color. No stimulation. Just…stuff.

A massive amount of stuff to have collected in less than a week.

Sitting in the rocker, he held the baby to his chest and rocked. Cradled her in his arms and rocked. She'd settle for a second or two and then start right back up again.

"Lay her on your lap," Tamara said. "On her stomach." Her purse was still on her shoulder. Her hand hurt, and looking down, she saw imprints of her keys in the flesh of her palm.

Flint pulled a blanket off the arm of the chair and did as Tamara said, settling Diamond Rose across his lap, continuing to rock gently.

"Rub her back," she suggested again.

The crying calmed for a second. Then another second. The baby burped, formula pooled on the blanket, and all was quiet.

Shaking, Tamara started to cry.

She had to get out of there.

In spite of the warmth seeping through the right leg of his jeans, Flint rocked gently, rubbing Diamond's back, while he wiped her mouth and pulled the soiled part of the blanket away from her. Her eyes closed, she sighed deeply and his entire being changed.

Irrevocably.

Almost weak with the infusion of love that swamped him, he knew he was never going to be the same. She was his.

He was hers.

Watching her breathe, he loved her more fiercely than he'd known it was possible to love.

And somehow Tamara Frost was connected to it all.

Tamara was gone when he finally made it back out to the great room. He'd known she would be. Putting Diamond in her Pack 'n Play, he flipped off the television still paused on a close-up of Michael Douglas with his mouth open, caught in midword. Then he gathered up the glasses of leftover iced tea, the half-eaten bag of popcorn and took them to the kitchen. Upon his return, he grabbed his laptop.

Settling back on the sofa, wanting to stay close to the baby, he did a search on medical degrees. They took an average of eight years to earn and then an average of four years of residency before a graduate could begin practice. A list of medical schools came next. He wanted the best. Decided on three and searched tuitions. Then he researched the average cost of living for a medical resident, did a calculation based on average cost of living increase each year, multiplying that by twenty-six, because, based on schooling, she'd be at least that before beginning a residency, and added the figure to his list.

His eventual total was about what he'd estimated when he'd been rocking his baby sister. But it was good to have solid facts.

He knew how much extra money he had to earn to fund Diamond's college account. She could be whatever she wanted. He was prepared for the most expensive, which was why he'd looked into medical schools. He checked the market next—something he did all day every day, using his cell phone when he didn't have access to his computer. Searching now for his own personal investments. There was always more money to be made.

And finding it was his talent.

He had all of half an hour before Diamond was crying again. Deciding it was about time, he tried to feed her. She drank for a couple of minutes and then turned her head. And kept turning it away whenever he tried to guide the nipple into her mouth.

So he rocked her. Laid her on her belly and rubbed her back. Walked with her out by the pool. Talked to her. Loved her.

And thought about Tamara. She'd fought her own demons that afternoon to help Diamond Rose. He couldn't remember a time other people had put themselves out on his behalf.

Except Howard Owens. He'd risked his own reputation to take Flint on eight years before. Flint hated that the man thought he'd been planning to stab him in the back.

Hated it, but wasn't surprised. That was the way his life worked. With his background, he was always suspect.

It was something he'd always known, even as a little kid.

And something he swore Diamond would never face.

Tamara had fought her own demons to hang around.

As he finally set Diamond down in a clean sleeper and with a full feeding of warm formula in her belly sometime after seven that evening, he pulled his cell phone out of his pocket. He'd changed into sweats and a long sleeved T-shirt and was sitting by the pool with a bottle of beer.

Tamara picked up on the second ring.

"I just wanted to apologize for this afternoon," he said as soon as she said hello.

"No apology necessary," she told him. "Seriously. I think what you're doing… Anyway, don't apologize."

There was no missing the wealth of emotion in her tone. He'd had a tough day with a cranky newborn, but he had a feeling Tamara's day had been immeasurably worse.

He did need to apologize. He'd been so certain he could help her—that somehow Diamond Rose would be the baby who'd help her heal from her loss, ease her pain—and with no real knowledge of the subject, he'd invited her into a hellhole.

He should just let her go.

He'd thought about it on and off all afternoon. And as he'd eaten his single serving of reheated lasagna for dinner.

He'd argued with himself and called her anyway.

There had to be *something* he and Diamond Rose could do for her.

"Maybe we should stick to having lunch for now," he offered, still at a loss.

If she even wanted to see him again. He wouldn't blame her if she thought he was too much trouble. He'd probably think so, too, if he were in her shoes.

Except he was beginning to understand that he had no idea how it felt to be in her shoes. Having children was a natural progression in life. Something most people took for granted. To be married and ready to start a family, to know you were pregnant, to be buying things for a nursery, making plans, and then to lose that child—he had no idea how any of that would feel.

And times four.

"Lunch would be good," she said, sounding a little less tense. "But dinner on Friday was good, too."

"Today wasn't."

"No."

"What did you do when you left?" Had she called a friend? How did she cope?

"I went to work." That he could completely relate to.

"Owens is closed on weekends."

"I have temporary clearance with security."

"Are you at the office now?"

"Yes."

He pictured her there. The building was quiet after hours. Peaceful. He did some of his best work when he was the only one on the floor.

Pictured himself there with her and actually got hard.

Either he was heading into the rest of his life or screwing up. At the moment, he wasn't sure which.

"You didn't get to finish your movie," he told her.

"You could tell me about it."

He heard invitation in her response and, settling back in his chair, beer in hand, he gave her a fairly detailed rundown of a movie he'd seen for the first time in junior high. He'd been in foster care, a six-month stint, and the family he'd been staying with had been watching old Charlie Sheen movies. The actor had just been hospitalized after having a stroke from a cocaine overdose. Flint's mother had been in jail at the time for possession of crack. The movie had a profound effect on him—establishing for him, very clearly, that ethics were more important than money.

But that money came a very close second. It had also given him his lifelong fascination with the unending opportunities provided by the stock market.

Not that he told Tamara all of that. With her, he stuck to the plot.

Until she asked him what it was that attracted him to the movie to the point of having watched it so many times. Then he told her about seeing it for the first time.

"Wow, that seems a bit callous to me," she said. "They knew why your mother was in jail, right?"

"I was certainly under that impression." He'd never asked.

"Did you say anything to them?"

"Nope." He'd known from experience that any questions from him would just lead to more lectures that he'd neither needed nor wanted. Or, worse, more scorn.

He was the bastard son of a drug user. Assumed to be like her, because how could he not be? He'd never experienced anything different. Not many good people were drawn to him.

"Did you know from the first time you saw the movie that you wanted to be a stockbroker?"

He sipped from his bottle. Chuckled. Pictured her in the converted closet they'd given her as an office and wished a glass of wine on her.

"I wasn't prone to lofty dreams," he told her. "I was curious about the market, but it didn't really occur to me that I'd have the opportunity to live in that world." She was easy to talk to. He couldn't remember the last time someone had been interested in him as a person.

Maybe some of that was his fault. He hadn't been all that open to sharing his life. Even with Stella. He'd shared his time. His plans. His future. But not himself.

He'd only just realized that…

"So when did you start believing in the opportunity?"

It took him a second to realize they were still talking about the stock market. He picked up the baby monitor on the table. Made sure the volume was all the way up. Diamond, who was just inside the door in her carrier on the table, had been asleep for more than half an hour.

"I had a minimum-wage job in high school, but I'd been earning extra money by going through trash, finding broken things, fixing them and then selling them. I'd made enough to buy a beater car and was saving for college. And I got to thinking I should look for things that were for sale cheap—you know, at garage sales—and then fix them up and resell them.

"I had quite a gig going until my junior year, when my mother got arrested again. I had almost enough saved to pay the minimum bail and went to a bondsman for the rest. I gave him an accounting of the books I'd been keeping with my little enterprise as a way of proving that I was good for the money. It's not like I had any real asset to use as collateral…"

He rattled on, as if he shared his story on a regular basis. Flint hardly recognized himself but didn't want to stop.

Talking to Tamara felt good.

"The guy was pretty decent. He paid the bond, without collateral, but told me he wanted me to check in with him every week, regarding my business intake. He helped me do my tax reporting, too. Supposedly it was just until Mom showed up in court and he got his money back, but I kept stopping in now and then, even after she was sentenced to community service and in the clear. He's actually the one who suggested I think about the stock market. He said I had a knack for making money. Turned out he was right."

He didn't hesitate to tell her the whole truth about this

aspect of his background, in spite of the fact he never did that. He guarded his private life so acutely.

"Did you ever go back and see him? After you made it?"

He hadn't made it yet. He wasn't even sure what "making it" consisted of these days. He'd thought that opening his own firm, having other brokers working for him, earning good money, would be making it.

"He retired and moved to Florida when I was a freshman in college."

And although Flint had given the guy his email address, had emailed him a few times, he'd never heard from him again.

"It was because of him that, years later, I started looking into offshore accounts," he told her. "He fronted money, which meant that he had to make money. He used to do a bit of foreign investing. He'd tell me about foreign currencies and exchanges and the money he'd make. He also talked about security.

"'Diversification equals security,' he'd say. If you keep all your assets in one place, and the place burns down, you're left with nothing. We like to think that our banks, at least the federally insured ones, are completely safe, and I feel that generally they are. But it doesn't hurt to have assets elsewhere, just in case of some major catastrophe—there can always be another crash like we had in 2008. It's not like it hadn't happened before that, too."

Okay, now he was reminding himself of Ross in an old *Friends* episode, going on and on about his field of paleontology and boring his friends to death.

"Sorry," he said, reining himself in. It felt as though a dam had burst inside him, which made him feel a bit awkward. But not sorry.

"Actually, this is the kind of thing I was after," Tamara

said. "Greater understanding of how the investment world works. But…I thought offshore accounts were illegal."

"Not at all. A lot of people use them illegally, because it's relatively easy to do. But they're not only completely legal, they're a financially smart decision. Especially for someone like me who invests internationally. You just have to report any earnings over ten thousand on your taxes."

"Do you do all your own taxes?"

"Yes." He did everything on his own, for the most part. He didn't like giving others the chance to make a mistake for which he'd be held accountable. "I meet with an accountant before I submit them, though," he added, "because the laws change every year."

Such a bizarre conversation. In a lot of ways, more intimate to him than sex.

And he'd started it.

"I'm sitting at the pool having a beer." He felt bad about that, considering his baby girl had sent Tamara running to work. "I wish you were here, enjoying it with me."

"I don't like beer."

"I have wine." It wasn't quite an invitation—he wouldn't do that to her, since there were no guarantees he could avoid a replay of this afternoon—but he had to open the door.

"Will it keep a few days?"

"Absolutely."

He asked her if she was free for lunch early in the week. They settled on Tuesday and Flint was grinning as he hung up the phone.

## Chapter Fourteen

Sunday was about as bad a day as she'd had in a while. First with the aborted visit at Flint's in the afternoon and then with the confirmation that he not only had an off-shore account but that he did his own taxes. Things that someone with something to hide might do.

Neither fact made him a thief. But the circumstantial evidence pointing in his direction, along with a lack of anything pointing in anyone else's, was certainly enough to lead her father to that conclusion.

Over the next week and a half, she worked like a fiend as an efficiency expert, finding several ways her father's company could save money. She also searched for any discrepancy that could place doubt or lay suspicion on anyone other than Flint. She found a few. She always did. But nothing that wasn't easily explainable or a product of human error or laziness. Someone cutting corners, but not for nefarious reasons.

She lunched with Flint twice that week. Spoke on the phone with him several times. Getting to know the boy he'd been, who'd grown to become the man he was. Sharing more of herself than she had in a long while. She talked about how—although she now loved her job—when she'd been younger, she'd really wanted to be a stay-at-home wife and mother. Old-fashioned though that might be, she'd thought that, having grown up with a wonderfully successful career mother and an equally successful businessman father, the ideal would be a home with someone always there. Protecting everything they all worked for. She wanted to add the personal touches to her own home that her parents' place had gained at the hands of hired help. But then, she worked a job that could largely be done from home, if she wanted it to be, so maybe that's why staying home seemed doable. All of the records scouring, the line by line accounts she studied, she could do that while the baby slept…

And she told him about her job, too. How she'd entered the efficiency field due to years of learning to live a focused life. How the career fit her, fulfilled her. How great she felt when she found bottom-line savings for her clients.

He'd asked, once, if she'd ever thought about trying one more time to have a family of her own. Her answer had been an unequivocal no.

She didn't see that changing.

Her heart had closed up at his question.

As the days passed, her father was getting more worried. He'd talked about calling Flint in, confronting him. But he knew that could be professional suicide. If the meeting backfired and Flint set out to prove he was innocent before Howard could prove he wasn't, any actions her father might take would expose the fraud at Owens.

He'd risk having everyone in the company finding out

they had a thief among them. He'd not only tip the thief's hand, but he'd jeopardize the company's overall security. Once word reached the investment world that Owens had an unsolved fraudulent situation in-house, it could be the end of everything her father had spent a lifetime working toward.

Howard needed the matter solved quietly. And quickly.

Tamara went to Flint's for dinner the following Saturday night, more intent than ever on learning whatever she could to help her father. But she got so distracted worrying about the baby waking up—and then, when she did, Tamara made herself sit out by the pool for the twenty minutes it took Flint to change and feed her—that she was of little use to Owens Investments that night.

Flint had been pleased for her, though, saying she'd done well, staying put instead of running out. She'd wanted so badly to be in there with him. Changing that baby. Watching him feed her.

And that unexpected desire had scared her to death.

She'd warmed under his emotionally intimate look.

And run out. Sort of. She'd had one more glass of wine—her second—and left before anything truly intimate could happen between them.

She dreamed about him that night. It was a change from her usual dreams about crowds of people holding babies, with only her arms empty. Or the vacant house she'd walk into to find every room a nursery that had been abandoned. Or the one where she'd gotten to hold Ryan for a few minutes and then he'd had to leave.

Dreaming about Flint was a welcome reprieve. And yet a problem, too.

One she figured she knew how to solve.

Calling Mallory Harris, she arranged to meet her friend for dinner the Monday night before Thanksgiving. They had a favorite spot not far from the Bouncing Ball—one that Mallory's ex-husband, who owned and worked in the office complex that housed the Bouncing Ball, didn't like. The food was all organic and salad-based. According to Mallory, Braden preferred full plates of food that stuck to his ribs.

Tamara had never met him. She was part of the life Mallory didn't share with her ex-husband.

"What's up?" Mallory asked as soon as they had glasses of Chardonnay in front of them.

"It's been a while since we hung out and—"

Mallory was shaking her head. With her dark hair trimmed to fall stylishly around her face and over her shoulders, Mallory was softly beautiful, even in clothes as plain as the Bouncing Ball jacket and jeans she'd worn to work that day. "I could tell when you called that something was up. Now, out with it. Did you run into Steve?"

"No." Mallory knew about Howard Owens's suspicions regarding Flint. Tamara had told her when she'd asked her friend to take on Diamond Rose. But there was so much more her friend *didn't* know, that she needed to know.

Mallory was just right for Flint. And he was right for her, too. Tamara really needed them to get together.

She'd almost kissed him the other night. Had been thinking about him sexually more and more over the past several days.

In spite of the baby who was part of his life.

He was making it too easy for her to be involved with him. The way he'd taken on full responsibility for Diamond impressed her. Plus the fact that he expected nothing from Tamara but distance where the baby was concerned.

She was getting in too deep. And, because of her father, she couldn't get out. Or not yet, anyway.

She was even starting to think she might not want to

get out at all. Which wasn't fair to anyone. That baby girl of his deserved—and needed—a full-time mother. Not one who stayed in other parts of the house or in doorways when Diamond was around.

She had to admit that Flint hadn't, in any way, intimated that he saw Tamara as anything more than a friend. Perhaps one with momentary fringe benefits.

He wanted her, too.

That was part of her problem. He was going to be asking. She'd managed to put him off without actually saying anything so far, but things were escalating between them. At some point he'd ask.

She didn't trust herself to say no.

Unless she thought her friend wanted him…

"It's Flint," she said. "He's such a great guy and I'm worried about him," she said, looking straight into Mallory's pretty blue eyes. "He's in that big house all alone, keeping up an eighteen-hour-a-day workload, being mother and father to that baby girl and—"

"You've been to his house?"

Yeah, she'd forgotten she hadn't mentioned that.

She nodded, but continued. "His girlfriend ditched him when he refused to give Diamond Rose up for adoption."

"Why were you at his house?"

Was Mallory jealous? That would be a good thing, right?

"I just… My father told me he's not going to press charges if it turns out that Flint's the one who's been stealing from him. And while I'm not excusing theft or fraud, I've seen another side to the man and—"

"When were you at his house?"

"I think you should ask him out, Mal."

Mallory sat back. "Me? Why? I thought you were going to tell me you were falling for him."

"He's got a baby."

"Yeah."

"You think I'm kidding about not going down that road again?" Tamara quipped.

"I think sometimes love is stronger than the things we believe."

"I can't even be in the same room with her for more than a few minutes without getting a cramped feeling."

"Exactly how many times have you been at his house?" Malory asked.

"You need to go out with him, Mal. You'll see what I mean. He's perfect for you."

"You really want me to ask him out?"

"I really do."

Mallory nodded. "He and I—we've talked some."

"And he's gorgeous."

Neither one of them was the type who fell for looks first, but looks didn't hurt.

"But I can't seem to draw him into any kind of conversation beyond caring for his daughter," Mallory said.

Sister. Technically, she was his sister.

Who'd grow up as his daughter.

And she assumed he'd told Mallory that. Probably had to present guardianship papers. None of which changed the fact that, for practical purposes, Flint was Diamond's father.

"He mentioned that he's planning to attend your Thanksgiving dinner at the Bouncing Ball. Said he's always gone out for dinner on Thanksgiving, usually invited clients, but with the baby... He doesn't want Diamond Rose to spend any holidays without family."

Tamara would be at her parents'. She'd told him that when he'd invited her to accompany him to Mallory's dinner—since she and Mallory were friends and all.

Things were just getting too complicated. She couldn't not go to her parents. And she absolutely could not take Flint there with her, Diamond Rose aside, even if she wanted to.

"You're thirty-three, Mal. You want a family of your own. And there's no reason you can't have ten children if you want them. But you need to get started."

"You seriously want me to ask him out?" Mallory asked again.

"At least try to spend some time with him at dinner on Thanksgiving. Ask him to help. He's a great cook."

"He's cooked for you?"

Tamara ignored that. "I think the two of you are perfect for each other."

"Seriously?" Mallory repeated, leaning forward, looking her in the eye.

"Yes." She didn't hesitate. This was the right thing to do. "Unless... I mean, depending on... My dad is still afraid that he's the one who stole from him."

"What do *you* think?"

Shrugging, Tamara took a sip of her wine. "The whole way he is with the baby and all, which has nothing to do with this, but... I don't see it," she said. "At the same time, there's absolutely nothing popping up on anyone else."

"So what do you do now? Hire a detective?"

"I tried to get my dad to do that. He's adamantly against bringing in anyone else. The thief, whoever it is, hasn't done anything in over a month. Dad had some special notification put on one of his passwords, and the second anyone signs in as him, he'll know. But he's hoping it doesn't come to that."

"How much longer are you going to be at the company?"

"I'm about done there." Which was another reason she had to get Flint and Mallory together.

"So you won't be seeing Flint anymore."

"I don't see him much at the office anyway. We're on different floors."

"Do you see him outside the office?"

"Only as a kind of informant," she said, confessing what bothered her the most. "I ask him questions about the business, in my efficiency expert role."

"But he thinks it's more than that."

"Just friends." Tamara sat back and drank some of her wine. Thought maybe they should look at their menus so their waitress would realize they'd be ready to order soon. They'd sent her off the first time she'd asked. "I swear. Nothing's happened between us. I'm not kidding. I've been thinking all along that you and he belong together. You'd love him if you got to know him. And you already love his little girl."

Which Tamara could never do.

Even if she wanted to try, she knew she'd go into emotional shutdown.

"You're falling for him."

"I am not! How could I? I only met him a few weeks ago."

"I knew I was in love with Braden the first night I met him."

A love that had been blown apart, for both of them, by the death of their five-month-old son. They'd been divorced for three years and had found a way to build a good, solid friendship between them.

"And now it's time for you to find someone else to love," Tamara said. "To share your life with."

"Maybe the one it's time for is you."

Mallory just wasn't getting it. "Are you not listening to me?"

"Actually I think that's exactly what I'm doing."

"You want me to open myself to possible feelings for a man who might be stealing from my father? And who has a newborn?" How could Mallory suggest such a thing?

"I want you to be honest with yourself." Mallory's words fell gently between them.

"I am," she insisted. "It's not like I can bring him home to dinner with the folks, Mal. And even if I could, I can't take on his baby. He already had a woman leave him because of Diamond Rose and he just doesn't deserve another kick in the teeth."

She started to tear up, took a deep breath and then said, "His whole life, Flint has done nothing but try, and give, and work hard. And his whole life, people have done nothing but desert him. It's not even like he lets that get to him. He's the least victimized person I've ever met. He'd doesn't get bitter. Or lay blame. He just picks up the pieces and keeps trying. Giving one hundred percent to whatever he does."

"It sounds to me like you know him pretty well."

"I've been…investigating him." At work. At lunch. In his home. On the phone. She'd spent more time with him than any other person since she'd been home.

"Really? Is that all?"

It *had* to be all.

For so many reasons.

But there was one that could convince Mallory…

"How do you suppose he's going to feel when he finds out that I'm Howard Owens's daughter? And that I've been spying on him because my father, his one-time mentor and current boss, thinks he's a thief?"

"You're in love with him, aren't you?"

"I've never even kissed the man!"

"You want to."

"I imagine half the women he meets want to."

"Maybe two-thirds." Mallory smiled. And then immediately sobered.

"I wish I knew what to tell you, Tamara. I just know that you don't get to choose love. It chooses you."

"It chose you and you're alone."

Tamara realized how cruel that sounded but Mallory didn't seem offended.

"I am," Mallory said. "Because human beings are fallible. Love gave Braden and me a chance. We failed it. But you're right. More than anything, I want to be married again, to have a family. And yes, I'm thirty-three. If I'm going to have a houseful of kids, I have to get moving on that. And here I sit. You know why? Because I can't *choose* to fall in love. I have to keep my heart open and wait for it to find me."

"You could go out more."

"I've been dating."

"Ask Flint out. Like I said, maybe love will choose the two of you."

If it was half as powerful as Mallory believed, it would choose her and Flint. It should! The match was obvious.

"I'm not doing anything with Flint Collins with you feeling the way you do about him."

"I don't feel any way about him except for horrible. I'm deceiving him, and he's such a great guy."

"Aside from possibly stealing from your father."

"Aside from that," she said. In spite of the number of times she kept reminding herself of the facts, such as they were, she just couldn't believe Flint was a thief.

Not considering everything he'd told her. Everything she'd seen in him over the past few weeks.

And as far as Stella went, Flint had seemed fully over her a week after they'd parted. He'd chosen Diamond Rose rather than her without looking back.

He'd changed his entire life for that baby. Because that was the kind of man he was.

And because it had been his mother's dying wish.

Because the baby was his only flesh and blood.

But what about before that? Maybe the Flint she'd gotten to know over the past weeks wasn't the man he'd been a month ago.

He'd had no idea his mother was pregnant, so clearly he hadn't seen her in a while.

He'd been hell-bent on starting his own business behind her father's back.

And what about those foreign investments he'd made on his own behalf, the risks he'd taken?

Maybe she just hadn't been looking in the right place for information. Maybe it wasn't information she needed.

Maybe what she needed here was a motive. Did it have something to do with Stella?

Was she the reason Flint Collins needed to steal money? Had she made him that desperate? And if not, had something else? If Tamara could find the answer to that question, she might be able to end this whole episode in her life.

Problem was, after her conversation with Mallory, Tamara wasn't sure she wanted it to end.

## *Chapter Fifteen*

Stella wasn't going away. Whether she was truly frightened of him now that she knew about his past or—more likely—just incredibly pissed off, she wanted a restraining order against him. No mutual agreement, nothing that could ever come back looking negative on her. All she wanted was him signing her damned paper, agreeing to release her family from any wrongdoing in perpetuity. And an order to stay away from her.

After almost two weeks of back and forth, trying to come to an amicable agreement, Flint's attorney called him the Friday after Thanksgiving and told him the only way to be free of the family was to fight them. In court. A date had been set for a hearing on the order for Thursday of the following week—on Diamond Rose's first-month birthday. Standing at the window in his office, watching the bustle of Black Friday shoppers on the streets below, he listened as his attorney highly recommended that he show up.

If he didn't, the order would automatically be put in place. Would become a matter of permanent record. In other words, if he didn't show up, he looked guilty.

Which meant that if he hoped to have any kind of long-term relationship with Tamara, even as just the close friends that was all she seemed capable of considering at the moment, he was going to have to tell her about the order.

It might be enough to push her out of his life.

He'd have to take that chance. He was done living with lies, hiding things because he was ashamed of them.

He was tired of being ashamed of his past.

The truth hit him so hard, he had to sit down. He was *ashamed* of who he was.

Almost as quickly as he sat, he stood again. The second he let life knock him to the ground, he gave it a chance to keep him there.

His much younger self had had the guts to stand up to the bullies on the bus and he sure as hell wasn't going to allow a selfish woman and her wealthy, powerful family to make him cower.

He had no reason to feel ashamed about anything. It was time to quit acting as if he did. Time to quit hiding the facts of his life.

Finishing with his attorney, agreeing to make the court date and authorizing him to go full-force ahead to have the order dismissed without cause, Flint hung up and called Tamara. She was working upstairs in her office, but she'd told him the night before, when she'd called after Thanksgiving with her folks, that she wouldn't be at the investment firm much longer. Her work there was almost finished.

She'd had a couple of offers. One local, one out of state. The out-of-state company was larger, but she hadn't yet confirmed either one. Hoped to be able to schedule both.

He hoped she'd be scheduling time for him, too.

"I hear there's an old-fashioned country Christmas-tree lighting at Pioneer Park in Julian tomorrow," he told her. "I've never been to a lighting, so I don't know what we'd be in for, but I was thinking it would be good for Diamond's first outing. Bright lights for her to focus on, and if she cries, we're outside in a noisy atmosphere. You want to come along?" He was taking a huge chance, maybe pushing her too fast. He went with his gut and did it anyway.

"I've actually been to that celebration before," she said. "Several times. It's nice. They have a lot going on. Santa. And other Christmas things. And…have you checked the weather? Do you know if it's going to be too cold to take her out?"

"The stroller has zip-up plastic walls and I've got a hat that completely covers her ears. And blankets."

He also had to tell her about the restraining order.

If they were going to move forward after her work at Owens Investments was done.

"So you hardly had a chance to talk to Mallory yesterday at the dinner, huh?" she asked out of the blue.

"There was another single father there, one she's apparently gone out with a time or two. While I like your friend, I had absolutely no interest in butting in where I clearly didn't belong."

"Would you have wanted to butt in if the other guy hadn't been there?"

Was she jealous?

Was it wrong of him to be smiling at that thought?

"If he hadn't, there wouldn't have been anything to butt into."

"Would you have asked her to the tree lighting if he hadn't been there? And the two of you had spent more time talking?"

"I just learned about it this morning," he told her. "I happened to see a sign on the way to work. If you don't want to go, you don't have to, Tamara. I'm not pressuring you. I'm just asking."

"It's not that I don't want to go…"

The problem was Diamond. He understood. So much more than she thought.

"She'll be in her stroller the whole time," he said. "And if there's an issue, I'll take her back to the car and handle it."

"Don't you think this seems more like a date?"

"It's whatever you and I decide it is. Just like our lunches. And dinners. Do *you* think it's too much like a date?" Maybe he was putting on some pressure, after all.

Maybe it was time.

"No. You're right, Flint. I'm making excuses."

"You don't have to go."

"I want to…" She sighed, hesitating.

"Then come with us."

"I'm scared."

"I know." He could support her. He couldn't take away her battle. Or fight it for her.

"Okay."

"You'll come?"

"What time?"

"It's about an hour's drive, so I'm guessing around five, being flexible in that I want to have Diamond freshly changed and fed right before I swing by to get you." He knew she owned a bungalow by the beach. He'd yet to be invited there. And he didn't even have the address.

"I'll meet you at your house," she said. "It's easier that way."

He'd prefer to deliver her safely to her door when they

got back, but let it go. She needed to be in control of her destiny. He was good with that.

And good with life in general, too. There would always be roadblocks. It was how he handled them that defined him.

Tamara had no idea what she was doing. Not really. Not deep down where it mattered. She'd told her parents, over a quiet Thanksgiving dinner the day before, that she'd befriended Flint for the purpose of spying on him for her father.

Neither of them had been thrilled with the news.

When she'd added that she liked him, and was struggling because of it, they'd looked at each other and frowned.

Her father had asked if that was how she'd known about the offshore bank account and, when she'd affirmed it, he'd asked her not to use a friendship to get any more information on his behalf.

He hadn't asked her not to be friends with Flint, although she figured from the concern on his face, and the hesitation in his tone, that he wanted to.

Instead, when she left, her parents had both implored her to be careful. They'd hugged her tight and she could almost physically feel their worry palpitating through them.

At no point during the day, not in a single conversation, had any of them mentioned a baby. Any baby.

And now here she was, sitting in Flint's car on the way to a holiday celebration, dressed in black leggings with black boots and a festive long black sweater with Christmas-tree embroidery. She wore Santa Claus earrings. Flint in his black pants and red sweater looked equally festive and she caught a glimpse of the baby's red knit hat when he'd loaded her carrier into the back seat. They resembled the stereotypical American family out to enjoy the season.

So not what they were.

It wasn't supposed to drop below forty degrees, but she'd dressed warmly.

At the moment she was sweating.

She hadn't turned around in the front seat, but she knew the baby was right behind her. Kept waiting for her to wake up. To need attention while Flint was driving...

"I have something to tell you." Flint's words brought her back to sanity fast. Was he going to confess that he'd siphoned money from his boss?

If he had, she needed to know. Needed all of this to be over.

And yet she didn't want it to end.

She felt trapped, with no way out. Or no way that would let her be happy when she got out.

For someone who had something to say, Flint was far too quiet. Maybe he wasn't ready?

"I have to be in court next Thursday to defend myself."

Everything stopped. It was far worse than she'd expected. He hadn't just stolen from her father? Someone else had pressed charges?

Where were her feelings of validation for her dad? Her rage?

All she could find was cold fear.

Disbelief.

"I told you about Stella—how I didn't tell her about my background..." He was continuing in the same calm tone. It took Tamara a second or two to catch up. There was an innocent baby right behind her. One who'd never have her own mom or dad, since her mother died without naming him, but had a brother who loved her as much as any parent could have.

"...she's taken out a restraining order against me. My attorney's been trying for two weeks to get her to sign a mutual stay away agreement, but she's more of a barracuda than I realized."

Focusing on the traffic along the freeway, taking herself outside something she wasn't handling well, Tamara juggled her thoughts.

"Stella claims you hurt her? That she fears for her safety?" She knew what restraining orders were for. Steve's sister'd had to get one against an ex-boyfriend.

Heaven help her, but there was no way she could believe Flint had threatened anyone, let alone a woman. He didn't deal with anger by attacking. He sucked it up.

She didn't have to see how livid he was to know that. She just had to listen to him, to see his tenderness, his unending patience with a crying child. And to know he'd given the mother who'd made his life hell a funeral, even though—as she'd later found out when she'd asked—he'd been the only one in attendance.

"The order actually reads that due to the fact that I hid from her who I really was, she fears for her and her family's safety."

"I thought you had to have proof of harm, or threat of harm, in order to get a restraining order."

"You only have to say you fear harm to get the initial order. The accused then has a chance to rebut the charge before the court and then the order's either granted or dismissed. If I don't go to court, it'll be automatically granted and become a permanent part of my record. Anytime someone did a background check, it would show up and I'd look like I'm an abuser."

"What a bitch." The words were out before she could stop them. She wasn't proud of them.

Flint's grin surprised her. "Thank you."

He didn't say any more about the situation and she didn't ask. He'd been honest with her, but she was lying to him every single second she was with him, by not telling him who she was. And she'd be breaking her word to her father if she did.

She felt like crap. She could blame Stella What's-Her-Name for wronging Flint, but she'd have to shoot recrimination at herself, too. Even after these weeks of getting to know him, she'd doubted him. The second he'd told her he was going to court, she'd assumed he'd done something wrong.

It could've been a simple traffic ticket he'd had to defend. That had never entered her mind.

And yet…she was drawn to him. To be with him.

So much it hurt.

## *Chapter Sixteen*

Public restrooms. Something else Flint had failed to consider in his new life. He was a man with a baby girl and he had to pee.

They'd been at the festival for an hour, had a couple of chai lattes and, together with the coffee he'd had before they'd left home, his situation was becoming critical.

He could take Diamond with him. Just wheel her right in. It wasn't like she'd know the difference.

But he would.

He didn't want her in a men's restroom, sleeping there close to the urinals or…in there at all.

His only other option was to leave her with Tamara. Which wasn't fair.

Urgency won out over fairness. "Can you just hold on to this while I pop in here?" he asked as they approached the cement building that housed the facilities. Not giving her much choice, he pushed the handle of the stroller in her direction and made his break.

Three minutes later, when he rushed back out again, his hands still wet from a brisk wash, they were exactly as he'd left them. Tamara hadn't moved. Taken a step. She was standing there, her hand on the stroller, staring at the men's restroom door.

And when he got close, he saw the tears in her eyes.

"I'm so sorry." He took the stroller, wheeled them out of the crowd and off to a bench not far from the festivities but far enough to give them privacy. With darkness having fallen, a chill had entered the air, although it wasn't cold enough to warrant the shiver he felt running through her as they sat.

"I should've thought ahead," he said, not sure what he could have done differently. Even without the latte, he'd have had to go at some point. It was what people did.

And what he'd need to do again before the evening was over.

"This isn't going to work, is it?" he asked her, not ready to give up but not willing to hurt her any more, either. "This is too hard for you."

She shook her head and, in a season filled with hope, he felt his dwindling once again. No matter how many times that happened, he never got used to it. It never got easier.

He wasn't going to try to convince her, though. He cared about her too much to watch her suffer.

"I'm the one who needs to apologize," she told him, turning so that she was looking him in the eye. "I need to try harder, Flint."

She'd lost four babies. Heartache wasn't something that could be brushed off or ignored. On the contrary, broken heart syndrome was a medically proved reality, as he'd discovered when doing some research on her situation.

"You're doing great, sweetie. I just..." What? He just what? He'd called her "sweetie." As if they were a couple.

She was still looking at him, all wide-eyed and filled with emotion. So close. He leaned in. She did, too. And their lips touched.

Maybe he'd meant it to be a light touch. A sweet good-bye to go with the endearment.

Maybe he hadn't been thinking at all.

What Flint knew was that he couldn't let go. Her lips on his... His world changed again and he moved his lips over hers. Exploring. Discovering. Exploding.

He felt for her tongue. Lifted his hand to the back of her head, guiding them more closely together. Felt her hand on his thigh.

Laughter sounded and it was a little too close. An intrusion, shattering the moment. He pulled back.

"I'm not going to apologize for that," he said, breathing hard. He glanced at Diamond, her stroller right there in front of them, the wheels lodged against his feet. The baby had been asleep for almost two hours. She'd be awake soon. Needing attention.

And Tamara...

She was looking at the stroller, too.

"I'm not going to run," she said. Maybe that made more sense to her than it did to him.

"Okay."

"There are a lot of things against us," she continued. "And chances are they'll win out eventually, but I'm not going to run away."

If the park staff had chosen that exact second to light the huge tree across the way from them, Flint's world wouldn't have been any brighter. He could hear "A Country Christmas" coming from the live band onstage in the distance and, for the first time, understood what people meant when they talked about the magic of Christmas.

"I'm very glad you aren't running away," he said aloud.

* * *

"I want to hold her so badly it hurts."

They were in the car on the way home. Tamara had tried to keep her mouth shut. There was no future for them; she had to let him go.

And couldn't bear the thought of it. Of deserting him.

Of him being deserted again.

"I'll help you try to hold her…"

She shook her head, arms wrapped tightly around her.

"We could start out easy," he said. "Just fix a bottle for her. Nothing else. See where that leads us."

Fix a bottle. She could do that. Maybe even do it without undue stress as long as she focused on something else while she completed the task. That wasn't how she usually did things; she typically focused on whatever needed doing immediately. But that wasn't what she needed here. She'd think about…what?

At the same time, she'd be paying attention to the amount of water to powder, of course.

"My dad bought Ryan a plastic baby fishing pole," she said, when fighting the inevitable didn't work. Babies always brought her to this place. "It's blue plastic with a red reel, and it has a big plastic handle that really turns and makes noise."

He glanced at her and then back at the highway.

Diamond had woken shortly after their kiss. He'd fed and changed her in the SUV while Tamara had wandered into a couple of nearby shops. After that, they decided to head out rather than wait for the big tree lighting.

"It's in the back of my shed." *Still in its plastic wrapping.*

"You never talk much about your parents."

Understandably, given the situation.

He didn't *know* the situation.

Guilt assailed her. She'd kissed him.

And she'd liked it.

Far more than she'd ever liked Steve's kisses.

What did that mean?

"Mom's a doctor." The darkness in the SUV made her feel safe. Secure.

Or maybe it was being with him.

"A cardiologist." Fitting. She was dying of heartache.

"And your dad?"

"He's into a lot of different things." He had investments in just about every field out there. "Computers, mostly," she said. She couldn't tell him the truth. But she wouldn't out-and-out lie any more than she had to.

She'd already told him she was an only child in one of their earlier phone conversations. They'd both been "onlys." She knew, from that same converation, that he didn't want Diamond to be.

"Have you told them about me?" he asked.

*Oh, God, don't strike me down in my sleep.* "Yes."

"And?"

"They're worried about my...well-being." She could be completely honest with that one.

"Surely they don't think you're better off alone."

"No, of course not. It's just been so hard...on them, too."

"Are they afraid of the possibility that you might get talked into trying again?"

*Trying again.*

Her chest tightened. The cords in her neck were taut. Her throat. What if she wanted that someday? Not simply to try again but...to try with Flint?

She shook her head.

She couldn't stretch the truth that far.

"I don't know," she finally said when she could.

"Do you think they want you to? Or hope you might?"

Looking out the car window, she thought about her mom and dad. "They've never said," she told him, but figured if they had, the answer would be no.

Just the thought of living through the months of waiting and worrying that would be involved—

Enough was enough.

And the three of them...they'd had enough.

The week following their trip to Julian was inarguably the best week of Flint's life so far. The only shadow at all was Stella's restraining order hearing and, in the end, it had been postponed. She'd asked for more time to prepare.

Not surprisingly, the judge had granted her request. Flint had had no say in the matter and only heard about the changed date when his attorney called to tell him he had to be in court the week before Christmas.

On the surface, not a lot had changed with Tamara. He still hadn't been to her home. She hadn't said why, but he could understand that it would be near impossible for her to have an infant in her most private space.

He would've been open to considering a lunchtime visit, but when she didn't suggest it, neither did he.

She'd wrapped up her work at Owens and while he'd liked knowing she was in the building, they hadn't crossed paths often enough for there to be a real difference in their time together. She'd taken the job in town, only a few miles from Owens, tentatively scheduling it for after the New Year. And on her last day in the office, he'd grabbed her out of view of all security cameras, telling her that knowing where the cameras were was a perk of spending so much time in the building—and then he kissed her. Soundly. So he could have that memory with him every single day he went to work.

She'd kissed him back fiercely. Telling him she wanted the memory to last.

They'd met for lunch four times that week. Twice they'd ended up in his Lincoln, making out. While it had been years since he'd even thought about kissing in a car, Flint was enjoying the slow pace of their relationship.

Tamara needed time.

He wanted her to have it.

If they went to her place, or his, they'd end up having sex and, as acutely as he needed that with her, he wanted it to be fantastic for both of them.

It wasn't going to be for her until she had some things worked out.

She'd been over for dinner twice and on Saturday afternoon to watch a movie. *ET* not *Wall Street*. One day at lunch they'd been talking about their favorite movies growing up and had decided to watch them all with each other. Her top three were *Mary Poppins*, *Annie* and *ET*. Other than *Wall Street*, his were *The Goose That Laid the Golden Egg*, *Rocky* and *Heaven Can Wait*.

Things were vastly different between them when they were around Diamond. The baby wasn't sleeping quite as much anymore. She'd happily spend time in her swing. Liked to be held for a while after she ate and before she went to sleep. She was also happy on a blanket on the floor for short periods, maybe ten minutes or so.

Tamara had mastered the art of bottle preparation. She'd taken over the sterilizing process, too, whenever she was there. She sat in a chair instead of on the couch with him when he was holding Diamond. And avoided looking in her direction at all other times.

Still, Flint took the week as a huge win.

She was trying.

And there was no doubt now that they equally craved their time together.

She came back on Sunday, bringing sushi for them to share while they watched a second movie. And then a third. They'd just finished *Heaven Can Wait*, a story about a young football player who'd left this world too soon, and she asked Flint about his mom. Not the bad stuff, she'd said, the good. She wanted to know all the things he'd loved about Alana Gold.

The things he wanted to pass on to Diamond.

If he was a guy who cried, he could have wept.

Over sushi, he asked her what she loved most about her parents. She'd liked that her mom never seemed like a doctor at home. She was just Mom.

Someone who worried too much. And was her greatest champion in the world.

"Dr. Frost," he said, anxious for the time to come when he could meet them. He'd been hoping by Christmas, but Tamara hadn't said anything.

"Her name's not Frost." The change in her tone was odd. Off. She looked like she had the day she'd picked up Diamond in his office.

Only different. Maybe worse.

"Your parents aren't married?"

"Yes. They are."

Sitting at the dining room table, with Diamond in her baby swing behind her, she dropped her California roll on the paper plate she'd brought.

He wasn't getting the problem. His baby girl hadn't made a sound. And Tamara couldn't see her to know she'd just smiled at him.

She'd been doing that a lot lately, this girl of his, smiling when she saw him.

"So your mother kept her maiden name?" he asked,

waiting to pick up another roll. He drank from the glass of wine she'd poured him.

She shook her head. "Frost's my married name." You'd have thought she'd admitted to some horrible crime, the way she'd said that. As if she expected him to be upset that she'd kept her ex's name.

A lot of women did that. For various reasons.

It was just a name.

"Okay."

Watching him for a second, she seemed to relax. She picked up her roll. And then another. Back to normal.

"So what *is* your maiden name?" he asked. He was planning to meet her parents at some point. He should know what to call them. Maybe even have their number in case of an emergency. They knew about him, so there was no reason he shouldn't have that information. "And do I call them Dr. and Mr. or—"

She'd gone completely white. Looked like she might be sick.

"Tamara? What's wrong, hon?" He stood, thinking he'd grab a cool cloth.

When she stood, too, he backed away from the table, giving her room to make it to the bathroom. But she wasn't going anywhere. She just stood there, facing him, looking... horrible.

"My parents are Dr. and Mr. Howard Owens."

## Chapter Seventeen

She hadn't meant to tell him. Oh, God, she hadn't meant to tell him. They'd been sitting there, eating sushi and having a great day, and she'd been so aware of the baby, needing to help care for her, and the awful lie had been there between them. He'd called her mother Dr. Frost. Dr. Steve's-Last-Name.

The lie had been too horrendous to keep to herself.

"Say something," she said.

He was standing there staring at her, frowning at her, completely confused.

"I... Did you just tell me that Howard Owens, my boss, is your father?"

She'd thought she'd felt every acute stab of pain there was to feel. She'd been wrong. The grip on her heart when she looked at Flint was different than anything she'd ever felt before.

"Yes." And if, judging by the expression on his face,

he was this put out about that part of it, he'd never be able to accept the rest.

She hadn't expected him to.

"You were working for your father."

"Yes."

He nodded. "Bill knew that."

She could almost hear his mind buzzing as he started putting the pieces together. But even Bill didn't know the whole truth.

"And your father told both of you not to say anything to the rest of the staff."

"Something like that." Exactly like that, except that he, in particular, had been singled out not to know.

"So when you interrupted us that first day… You're the real reason I kept my job. You talked to your father—"

"No!" She shook her head. "I mean, I did say something, but he'd already decided to keep you on. He'd met with you by then. You'd already signed the noncompete agreement."

"Which you thought was a good idea."

"I did."

He nodded, his brow clearing a bit. She wished she could feel relief but she knew better. Her lips were trembling. Her hands and knees, too. Tamara slid back onto her chair.

"I can see why your father wanted you to do your work without anyone knowing you were his daughter. People would be more honest with a stranger who had no ties to their boss."

She wanted to nod. He was right—to a point.

She could sense that he was taking hope. Saw him working everything out in his mind.

It was an endeavor doomed to fail before he'd even begun.

The sound of the swing, back and forth, back and forth,

click, click, played a rhythm in her mind. Soothing her. She concentrated on that. Focused on it.

"Did you really tell them you're seeing me?"

"Of course."

There were no longer any creases on his brow.

"And they were okay with it?"

"They didn't tell me not to." That point was key. He had to know they hadn't rejected him—despite believing he might have stolen from them. She'd even go so far as to say, "They're supportive of whatever choice I make where you're concerned."

"But they're worried."

She'd already told him that much. She nodded.

"Your dad knows about my past. And about Diamond Rose."

Of course he knew. Flint had informed Howard about the baby himself.

He frowned again. "When I asked you to give me time to tell him...did you?"

"Yes."

His brow cleared. If she didn't know better, she'd start to take hope herself. As it was, she wanted to throw herself in his arms, beg his forgiveness and have wild, passionate sex.

She wanted to focus on him. On them. All the issues separating them be damned.

At the same time she wanted to run, but didn't trust her knees to carry her away from him.

"So...now that the cat's out of the bag," he began, "how about we pack up the girl here and stop over to see them? I know Howard generally spends his Sunday evenings during football season in front of the seventy-two-inch screen he had installed in your parents' family room."

"You've seen it?" She gulped. Buying time she didn't have.

"Of course not. He doesn't expose his employees to his family—and vice versa. You'd be the first to know that."

She nodded.

"So…give them a call. Let's get this over with." His tone was light. His expression wasn't, but it was filled with the warm light of…caring she'd become addicted to seeing from him over the past weeks.

She shook her head.

Flint sat on the edge of the seat closest to her then leaned forward, taking both of her hands in his. "I know there's a lot we still have to face, sweetie. Just as I understand why they're so concerned for you. Let me assure them that I know what's going on. That I have no intention of asking you to do anything if you aren't ready. Even if you're never ready. Let me set their minds at ease."

She couldn't do that. But how to tell this wonderful man—the man she seemed to have fallen in love with—that nothing was as it seemed.

She loved him? Nothing like going for the bottom line when everything was falling apart.

Mallory had been right. She'd known how Tamara felt before Tamara knew it herself.

She wasn't surprised by that.

"You owe it to me," he said next, his tone still light, grinning as she looked up at him. "I have to see him at work tomorrow, knowing that he knows but that he doesn't know I do." He rolled his eyes. "Whew. This is complicated."

He made her smile.

Which made her cry.

She loved him.

And she was about to hurt him so badly.

She loved him.

And she was about to lose him.

\* \* \*

Getting over the initial shock, Flint was filled with undeniable energy. Ready to forge into the future. Taking Tamara in his arms, understanding her emotions as she finally told him a secret he'd had no idea she'd been keeping, wanting her to know that he understood and held no hard feelings. He rubbed her back. Buried his face in that glorious auburn hair. Inhaled her soft, flowery scent.

If ever he could have scripted a life for himself, it would be this one.

He'd known Howard Owens had a daughter, but he hadn't heard much about her. She'd gone to college. Gotten married. He'd never heard anything else.

He certainly hadn't known that Howard had lost four grandchildren before they were born. The man he'd thought unemotional to the point of impassive had gone out and bought his unborn grandson a fishing rod. Hard to accept that one—and yet he'd always admired Howard, had wanted to be like him. Other than the older man's penchant for playing it safer than Flint's gut told him to do.

And now…here he was, in an incredible relationship with the man's daughter. Howard knew, and hadn't told his daughter to run in the opposite direction.

"Flint…"

Sniffling, Tamara pulled away from him. Wiped her eyes. She wasn't smiling.

He stilled. "What's wrong?"

Tears welled in her eyes again as she looked up at him.

He didn't start to sink back to reality, though, until she took another step back. Bracing himself, he waited.

No point in reacting until you knew what you were reacting to.

"There's more. And I want you to know, right up front, that I don't care anymore."

Now he was confused. "Care about what?"

Was she telling him she had no feelings for him? He found that hard to believe. She had to be running scared because of Diamond.

A problem, to be sure. But they could work on it.

There had to be a way…

"Whether or not there's any truth to my father's suspicions. I *should* care. But I don't. I told him that on Thanksgiving Day." She stopped. Took another couple of steps backward, toward the great room where she'd left her purse.

He was watching her leave him.

He didn't get it.

"I told him I wasn't sure how much longer I could go without telling you…"

What, that she was Howard's daughter?

And what were Howard's suspicions? Flint had already admitted he'd been in the process of opening his own business. That had all been before Diamond. Before Tamara.

"What did he say to that?" he asked because he couldn't come up with anything else.

"He understood that I had to do what I had to do."

"But he didn't want me to know?"

She shook her head.

Okay, so all was not as he would've scripted it.

"He wanted proof, first."

*Proof?* Flint needed her back in her chair, across from him, eating sushi. He had no idea how to make that happen.

"He's not going to press charges," she said. "He told me so. Especially not if it's you. You need to know that…"

*Press charges? What the hell?*

No.

Grabbing the back of the chair with both hands, he

stood calmly. His life was what it was. Always had been. Maybe it always would be.

And he'd deal with it.

"Why don't you leave out all the preliminaries and tell me what your father thinks I've done."

"Someone's been siphoning money from the company."

"And he thinks it's me."

She nodded.

Her tears didn't faze him. The stricken look on her face didn't, either. He noted both, but was somewhere else entirely now. He was in his own world, where there was just him. Knowing that he had what it took to deal with whatever was in front of him.

First was finding out the facts. All of them.

"And you've known this how long?"

"It's why I was working at Owens," she said, exposing more and more of a nightmare he'd thought he'd already seen in its entirety. "As an efficiency expert, I'd have access to everyone and everything in the company. He wanted me to see what I could find out."

"You were his spy." His mind was working. The rest of him was dead to the world. Shock, maybe.

Survival, certainly.

"Yes." He respected the fact that she didn't spare herself. Didn't lie to him.

Ha! Irony to the hilt. She'd been lying to him since the moment they'd met.

A flash of that day in Bill's office came to him, along with a stab hard enough to stop his airflow. "Bill knew."

She shook her head. "Well, he knew who I was, but he doesn't know why I was really there. No one does, except my mom and dad and me."

She hadn't been sent to him by Alana Gold. Or for any

good reason. Her presence hadn't been a coincidence; he'd been right about that. But her purpose...

"He wanted you to look into me in particular," he said aloud. "Your interest in me—it wasn't real..."

Thinking of her there, in his home, with Diamond Rose, he wanted to puke up the sushi he'd just consumed.

He wanted her gone.

"I wish that was true!" Her words came out on a wail. "I wish to God my interest was nothing more than a way to ease my father's worry. Instead, I fell in love with you. When he told me he wasn't going to press charges, it was as though this huge flood of relief opened up inside me and I've been a mess ever since."

*She fell in love with him.*

Right. She expected him to believe that?

"I'm guessing you didn't find anything to convict me?" he asked almost dryly, although he was starting to sweat in earnest.

If he'd made a mistake along the way, and they were going to make it look like he'd purposely cheated the firm...

Who'd believe him?

"Obviously, I'm not a criminal investigator, but I couldn't find anything on anyone," she said. "But circumstantially, you're the most suspect."

*Criminal* investigator.

Sweat turned to steel. No way was he going to jail!

He would not lose Diamond.

His mind took over. "Circumstances meaning my past? My background?"

"Your offshore accounts."

The night he'd been talking to her about the *Wall Street* movie. He'd been falling in love. She'd been taking notes to betray him.

He'd think about that another time. If an occasion arose that required it.

"I know of four other brokers in the firm who have them. What else?"

"Your spending habits changed."

"I had a rich girlfriend I was trying to impress, and money I'd saved for a day when I had someone to spend it on."

She didn't deserve any explanations, but he was *not* going to jail.

"You were opening your own firm behind my father's back."

"I intended to do just as he'd done when he opened his firm. Once I knew the legalities were in place and it was actually going to happen, I intended to go to him with my plan. I was about a week away from that when I got word that my mother was dead. I'd planned to give Howard the opportunity to send a letter to all my clients, naming a broker in my stead, and move on. If any of them found me elsewhere and chose to follow me of their own accord, then I'd continue to service them. Instead, I heard from Jane in Accounting, that someone found out—I don't know who or how—and I heard that Bill went to your father with a version of the truth that made me out to be unethical."

And clearly Howard had believed that version.

She hadn't stepped back any farther. He was ready for her to do so. To keep stepping back until she was gone from his home. From his life.

He wanted to forget ever knowing her.

Forget that he'd ever thought her beautiful...

Her eyes flooded again. Like a sucker, he'd fallen for that compassionate look in her eye. And the fear she'd exposed to him.

But no more.

"Jane is the one who started the rumor. She found out what you were doing from a friend of hers who works at the office of the Commissioner of Business Oversight. She knew you worked at Owens, where Jane works. Jane's the one who told Bill. Why Bill spun the news when he told my father, I have no idea. A charity account was used to run the money through." She spoke as though she was giving testimony.

Jane had betrayed him! He'd thought the grandmother of four liked him.

"You were the only broker who knew the account number because, for a time, you donated your expense checks to it as a tax write-off."

"All three of the company directors, and your father, as well as at least one person in Accounting, not Jane, has access to that account."

She could keep throwing things at him. He'd done nothing wrong. Knowingly, at least. But it was clear to him that she was prepared to keep talking. He had to know whatever she knew, to find out what he was defending himself against. He was careful to keep his tone as level as hers. To converse. Not to shut her down.

"The broker who took the money used various office computers at all different hours of the day—always computers that aren't within view of security cameras."

A flash of memory from the past week visited him. The quip he'd made about knowing corners that were out of view of security cameras when he'd kissed her.

"You were spying all along?"

She neither confirmed nor denied that one.

Her list—and her father's—could be convincing. He was seeing the picture she was building.

And yet…

He was *not* going to jail. He would not abandon Diamond Rose as he'd been abandoned. He'd give her up first.

The baby, not three feet from him, slept obliviously. He was thankful for that. She didn't know. And if he had his way, she'd never know.

"Whoever it was signed in under my father's account."

"Then why don't you look at someone who knows his password?"

"He thinks you do."

"I don't. Go talk to Bill Coniff, since you're so fond of him. He has the password. Maybe he gave it to someone."

"How do you know Bill has it?"

"I've seen him use it," he told her. "A couple of times when we needed something critical and your father was out. I'm assuming the other two directors have it, as well."

"You've actually seen Bill sign in to my father's account?"

He saw where this was going. If he'd seen Bill type the password, then it would stand to reason he could retype it himself.

"I was on the other side of the desk. I didn't see him type. I just know he accessed the information we needed."

Tamara stared at him. They were done.

"Look, Bill's the one who told your father that I was starting my own business, spinning it to look like I was planning to contact my clients and steal my book of business. When, instead, upon hearing the rumor from Jane, he could have just come to me. Given me the chance to go to your father. And Howard believed Bill's take on what I was doing, without discussing it with me. And he apparently still believes I'm guilty of stealing from the company. Just as he's going to believe whatever else Bill tells him. Including that he gave me your father's password. Or that I was on his side of the desk and saw him type it."

He could see the evidence piling up. Bill would testify that he'd seen Flint use the password. It would be Bill's word against his, and even a kid could figure out who a judge would believe on that one.

Tamara wiped her eyes. Picked up her purse. "I'm sorry, Flint. I—"

"Just go."

"I'm going to do everything in my power to clear your name," she said. "That's what I've been trying to do—"

"You could've just asked me if I'd stolen money from your father's company."

She nodded. "If you ever need anything…"

He'd know who not to call.

Flint watched her walk out of his life and then calmly locked the door behind her.

*Merry Christmas.*

He allowed that one bitter thought and then got busy.

He'd do what it took. Just as he always had. He was going to *be* someone.

Not for Alana Gold. Not even for himself.

For Diamond Rose.

## Chapter Eighteen

*Four days later*

Bill Coniff, who, it turned out, had a gambling problem, resigned from Owens Investments and quietly disappeared. After signing a full confession, as well as other documents at the behest of Howard's team of lawyers, making sure he couldn't malign Owens Investments, the Owens family, or ever again work as a trader in the State of California. In exchange Howard didn't press charges because it was best for the company not to have it out there that they'd had a traitor in their midst.

Tamara discovered that Bill hadn't originally planned to frame Flint; at first he'd truly been pissed that the guy was leaving. But not because of Howard. Because of himself.

As Flint's boss, he got a percentage of the money Flint made for the company. But then he'd figured out that Howard knew about the siphoning of money thanks to an extra-long meeting Howard had with his accountant after the company taxes had been done. A meeting that Howard hadn't shared with his top three people, as he usually did. And, after which, Howard had asked the three of them about their use of the charity account.

Bill had known by then that Flint was leaving. He'd known, too, that with Flint's expertise, plus his background, he could easily frame him for his own wrongdoing. He'd seen a way out. And had been desperate enough to take it. And then Flint had changed his mind about leaving. He'd needed Flint gone. His chances of getting Howard to believe him would not only be much stronger that way, but he'd been afraid that, once accused, Flint would figure out for himself who was guilty. Bill had gambled on the fact that Howard would believe him over Flint if it ever came to a "his word against Flint's" situation.

As much as Tamara wished differently, Flint wasn't around to know about any of it, including Bill's leaving, or the agreement between him and Owens Investments.

Sometime after she'd left him that Sunday night, he'd packed up Diamond Rose and gone to Owens Investments, clearing out his office and leaving his key in an envelope under Bill Coniff's door. Howard had told her it had looked almost as though he'd purposely left behind a trail of his actions by staying within security-camera range anytime he could. He'd packed his office in the hallway, carrying things out and loading them into bags he'd brought with him, one by one. Showing the camera everything he was taking.

In tears, Tamara had asked for a copy of the tape. She watched it several times in the days that followed, sometimes staring only at Flint. And at others, finding herself looking at the precious baby she'd once held.

Once.

She started the job she'd accepted early and worked long hours so she'd be finished by Christmas. Focusing on the task and not on herself. She knew how to cope with grief.

And when the nightmares woke her, she lay in bed and replayed her time with Flint over and over—starting with the first meeting between her and her father in Howard's office, to that last horrendous half hour at Flint's house.

Working for her father, virtually undercover, to preserve the integrity of his business had not been wrong. Hanging out with Flint…that didn't feel wrong.

Falling in love, though? Completely inappropriate. And yet if Mallory was right, she didn't get to choose love, love chose her.

So what the hell? She'd been chosen to have a life of misery? Of unrequited love? First for the four children she'd lost? And now for Flint?

And little Diamond.

Even from a distance, that little girl had found her way through Tamara's defenses.

Tamara was crying too much again.

She spent a lot of time with her parents. Going over lawyers' paperwork with them as they moved immediately on getting Bill Coniff out of their lives. From start to finish had taken four days.

And now, here she was, on Saturday, two weeks and two days before Christmas—almost done with the current job and another beginning in the new year, with holiday functions to attend with her parents and shopping to do— walking up to Flint's front door like an idiot.

She knocked, having no idea what she'd say to him. She'd already said it all. She'd explained. She'd taken full responsibility. She'd also told him she didn't give a damn whether or not he was guilty. That she'd known her father wouldn't press charges. That he'd be okay. She'd told him she'd fallen in love with him.

Nothing she'd said had mattered. She understood that, too.

Knocking a second time, she told herself that her behavior was bordering on asinine. But she had to see him. To let him know he was off the hook—they'd found their thief. Just so he didn't worry that, on top of Stella's order, he had another possible court situation to face.

And she needed to know he was okay.

Maybe find out where he was working, so she'd know that he and Diamond were secure.

She'd already called Mallory, knew that Diamond Rose was still coming to day care on her regular schedule. Had been there the day before.

She knocked again.

Flint didn't answer any of her knocks.

With the garage door closed, she couldn't tell if he was home or not.

One thing was clear, though. If he was inside, he'd seen who was on his porch and definitely didn't want anything to do with her.

She had to honor that choice.

She just hadn't expected it to hurt so much and couldn't contain the sobs that broke out as she turned and walked away.

Flint heard from Howard Owens every day that first week after his last meeting with Tamara. He didn't pick up, leaving them with one-way conversations via voice mail. One way—from Howard to him. He didn't return any of the calls. Howard was requesting an in-person sit-down. He wanted Flint to stay on at Owens Investments. He never mentioned the theft, or his suspicions, not even on the first call Monday morning, when it had become known that Flint had cleared out. By midweek, his messages changed only to add that he'd put out the word to Flint's clients that, due to having just become a father, he was taking a week or two off. Howard was personally handling Flint's entire book of business.

Flint might have called him back to tell him to go to hell. If he'd been a bitter man.

Even when Owens implored him, he ignored the summons.

And when he sent his spy daughter to Flint's home to plead his case? Especially then. He was fighting for his very life. Something neither of them would know anything about.

It was possible he would've capitulated after a full week's worth of calls, but on the Tuesday after the truth about Tamara had come out, while Flint was home alone researching his next career path, he'd received another court notice.

Not from Stella this time.

Much worse than Stella.

Lucille Redding, Diamond's paternal grandmother, a woman no older than Diamond's mother, was petitioning for custody of his little girl. No one had told him Diamond's paternity had been discovered, let alone that there was a paternal family.

He'd called Michael Armstrong, his attorney, immediately. Faxed the petition over to him. Asked about the repercussions of taking his baby sister and disappearing from the country. Hadn't liked that answer at all.

Michael had told him to sit tight and let him do some investigating.

Flint had cashed in some of his more lucrative personal investments, moving the money to his offshore account.

He called his attorney again, filling him in on the news Tamara had given him on Sunday, assuring him that he absolutely had not taken any money from anyone in any kind of illegal capacity. Michael told Flint he believed him.

He wouldn't blame the guy for having doubts. But he was paying him to keep them to himself.

Instructed once again to sit tight, Flint packed a couple of emergency suitcases, one for him, one for Diamond Rose, just in case, storing them in the trunk compartment in the back of his Lincoln.

For the rest of that day he'd researched career options and tried not to hear Tamara's voice in the back of his mind. He played music. Turned it up louder. Left the news on in the background, watching the stock channel on cable.

She didn't love him. Truth was, she'd been so hurt, she was probably incapable of truly loving anyone, other than maybe her parents.

He'd put Diamond to bed in her carrier that night, keeping it on the bed with him, a hand on her, on it, at all times. If he hadn't read that it was unsafe to have the baby sleeping right beside him—read about the danger of rolling over in his sleep and suffocating her—he'd have snuggled her little self right up against his heart, where he intended to keep her forever. Safe from a world that would judge her just because of who she'd been born to. And where she'd been born.

As if she'd had a choice about any of that!

Michael called Wednesday morning just as Flint was pulling out of the Bouncing Ball Daycare.

Turned out that Alana Gold had had an affair with a twenty-eight-year-old male nurse, Simon Redding, an army reservist working in the prison infirmary. Simon had fallen in love with her and, according to what he'd told his mother, Alana had loved him, too.

Which was why Alana had refused to name him as her baby's father. She'd been protecting him from prosecution.

At his mother's insistence, Simon had volunteered for deployment shortly after he'd slept with Alana, to get himself as far away from temptation as possible. He'd died in Afghanistan just after Thanksgiving and his mother, honoring the love her son had said he'd felt, and knowing he could no longer be hurt by it, had tried to contact Alana. To visit her.

Only to learn that she'd died in childbirth. That the affair could have resulted in a baby girl.

She was requesting a DNA test to prove that her son was Diamond's father.

And, assuming the test was positive, would be suing for custody. She was married. To a colonel in the air force. Was a schoolteacher. Simon had been their only child.

They had the perfect family unit in which to bring up a little girl.

On Friday he'd received a court order to provide Diamond's DNA.

And as early as Monday or Tuesday, he could be faced with having to set up a time to make her available for a grandparent visit.

He wasn't leaving the house at all that day or the next. He and Diamond were going to lie on her blanket on the floor and watch children's movies. He was going to rock her. Feed her. Bathe her. Take pictures and video of all of it.

And come Monday, in spite of the fact that he had a pending restraining order against him, an ex-boss who suspected him of theft, no job and had been suspected of helping his convict mother finance the drug business that had put her in prison, he was going to fight like hell to keep Diamond and him together.

He could be a good father. And a good brother. Both at once. He knew that now.

No one was going to love her more than he did.

No one but him could raise her to understand the good that came from being Alana Gold's child. Or teach her about the good that had been in Alana herself.

Diamond wasn't just a convict's daughter. She was the daughter of a woman who, though afflicted with the disease of addiction, had loved fiercely. Laughed often. Who'd listened to understand. Who'd always, always, come back.

And who'd taught him how to live with determination, not bitterness. To stand instead of cower. To carry dignity with honor even when others tried to strip it away.

She'd made him the man he was.

It was up to him to teach Diamond all the value to which she'd been born.

Because she wasn't just going to *be* someone.

She *was* someone.

On the Tuesday of that next week, fourteen days before Christmas, Tamara joined Mallory at the Bouncing Ball after work to help her friend put up Christmas decorations. Saying that putting the tree up too early made the little ones anxious, Mallory always decorated for two weeks and two weeks only. If the day after Christmas was a workday, she came in Christmas night to take down the decorations.

Tamara had promised herself that she wasn't going to mention Flint or Diamond Rose. Nor was she going to look for any evidence that either of them had been there.

If Flint wanted her to know anything about them, he'd call her.

He'd have answered his door.

Her spying days were over.

Which made it a bit difficult when, after they'd hauled

the artificial tree out of the back of the storage closet, straightened its branches and were just starting to string lights, Mallory said, "Flint offered to stay and help do this."

Mallory knew Tamara wasn't friends with Flint anymore. Knew he'd quit her father's company. Why on earth was she...?

And then it hit her. Flint and Mallory.

Standing on one side of the tree, she passed the long strand of stay-cool lights over to Tamara, who wrapped the two top branches in front of her and handed them back. Mallory's tree always had lights on every single branch to make up for the lack of ornaments that she said just tempted little ones to reach out and touch.

Tamara had insisted that Mallory and Flint would be perfect for each other.

Had thrown him at Mallory.

Her pain at the thought of them together was no one's fault but her own.

"I figured Braden would be here," she said, bringing up Mallory's ex only because she'd promised herself that she wouldn't talk about Flint behind his back. But lying to herself was really no better than lying to Flint, although the truth was that she couldn't bear to hear Mallory talk about him.

Mallory passed the lights back to her.

She didn't know what she'd do if Flint and Mallory became a couple.

Move back to Boston probably.

Keep in touch with Mallory for a while by phone, wish her well from the bottom of her heart, then slowly fade away from them completely.

It was the right thing to do.

"Braden's always helped you in the past," she continued just because she'd already started the conversation. Taking off the section she'd just wrapped when the lights all fell onto the same branch, she tried to rearrange them.

"He's out on a date tonight."

Oh. She passed the lights back to her friend. "Is she someone new?"

"I have no idea. I didn't ask." Mallory's tone said she didn't care. Tamara wasn't sure she believed that. She'd never completely understood the relationship between Mallory and Braden.

"How about that guy you were seeing at Thanksgiving? What was his name? Colton something? Is that going anywhere?"

"No. My call. Not interested." Mallory returned the lights to her.

So it was Flint, then. Leaning down as they reached their way along the tree, Tamara covered a wider section of branches.

She should be glad to know that Flint and Mallory might find each other. She loved both of them and neither deserved to be alone. And yet…what kind of woman did it make her that she couldn't bear the thought of the two of them together?

"Flint's in a real bind, Tamara."

With the string of lights hung, Mallory plugged it in, making the room glow with the overabundance of multicolored twinkling lights. Tamara barely saw them.

"What's wrong?" she asked. Was it Stella? His court date wasn't until the following week. But the woman could have showed up somewhere he'd been and then called the police to report that he'd been near her.

"Please don't tell him I told you, but if there's anything you or your family can do to help…" Mallory bent to the box of decorations, hauling out plastic wall hangings. Tamara recognized the long faux mantel she was unfolding, on which Mallory would hang stockings for each of the kids, with their names on them.

"What's wrong?" she asked again, more tension in her voice than she'd ever used with Mallory before.

"He just doesn't strike me as a man who'd ever ask anyone for help, at least not that he couldn't pay for and..." Mallory was bent over the box again.

"Mallory!"

Her friend stood, a garland of bells in hand, facing her.

"It goes against everything in me to talk about a client but...he might lose Diamond Rose, and if he at least had a job..."

Heart pounding, Tamara could hardly breathe. Lose Diamond Rose?

She hadn't told Mallory he'd quit Owens Investments. Apparently he'd done that himself.

"My father's been calling him every day for a week, trying to get him to come back," she said. "He doesn't pick up and won't return his calls. What's going on?"

Flint could lose his baby?

Because of Stella's order?

"Her paternal grandparents have come forward, demanding a DNA test, and they're suing for custody."

Tamara fell into the chair closest to her. A tiny, hardbacked one. Mallory told her what Flint had been going through since she'd last seen him, at least the parts he'd shared with her. And only because he'd had to give Mallory's name to the courts, who'd be contacting her as Diamond's caregiver.

"Her father's younger than Flint." Tamara said the only thing she could focus on that didn't make her feel like she was suffocating.

Wow.

Oh, God.

"The grandparents are in their late forties, young enough to participate fully in her activities as they raise her. They've been married for twenty-five years, have professional jobs and not so much as a speeding ticket. Their son was a nurse and in the army reserves. His only apparent mistake in life was falling in love with Alana and having sex with her while he was working in the prison infirmary."

Mind speeding ahead now, Tamara stood as a list of supposed sins against Flint sprang to mind. She knew them well because she and her father had listed them as reasons to suspect him of theft.

She knew how easily that list could convince someone against him. And she and her dad hadn't even had the restraining order to include in the mix.

Add to that, he'd just left his job—walking away from all the people who'd been loyal to him for almost a decade, some more than that, who would've been able to testify on his behalf. Including his client list.

He had no one. No family. No girlfriend. No one to stand up and tell the court what a travesty it would be to take that baby away from him.

"He's a single man without a job," Mallory said. "I was thinking, if your father took him back, at least that issue would be solved... I didn't know he was already trying to do so."

And Flint hadn't returned Howard's calls. Because the one thing Flint had never learned was to rely on others. To allow himself to need anything he couldn't provide for himself. Or pay for.

Because he could never believe that anyone would help him.

He'd probably thought, in spite of Howard's assurances

otherwise, that her father was trying to get him to talk about the missing money. He'd have no way of knowing that Bill had admitted his gambling addiction, confessed everything. Some of it was confidential and couldn't be told, and the rest... Her father wanted to apologize to Flint in person, man to man. Eye to eye.

"I'm sure he won't value his pride over Diamond Rose," she said. "He can't. Especially once he finds out what's been going on." Apologizing to Mallory for abandoning her, she grabbed her bag and ran out.

She had to get to her father. To convince him to do whatever he had to—beg at Flint's front door if it came to that, or camp out in the Bouncing Ball parking lot until he showed up there—to give him his job back, whether he wanted it or not.

That was for starters.

What she could do after that, she hadn't figured out.

She just knew she had to focus. Get to her father.

And figure it out.

## Chapter Nineteen

The last thing Flint had expected to see as he was coming out of the Bouncing Ball Wednesday morning was Howard Owens standing beside his Lincoln.

"I have nothing to say to you," he said, getting close enough that the fob in his suit pocket unlocked the door. He rattled off the name of his attorney, telling Howard to say anything he had to say to Michael.

He got in his vehicle and pushed the button to lock the doors behind him.

DNA tests were expected that day or the next. They could've been in as early as Monday. Flint was considering every night he had with Diamond as a gift at this point.

Living from moment to moment.

And planning for a future with his baby girl, too. He had to, if he was going to stay sane.

He had to, to give Michael something to present to the judge. Something that could stand up to practically perfect grandparents.

About to put the SUV in drive, he glanced out the windshield and stopped. Howard was standing there, right in front of the vehicle. Arms crossed.

Challenging him.

The man was in his fifties, graying, but every inch the fit and muscular man he'd been when Flint had first met him.

Flint couldn't be intimidated anymore. He'd had enough. He reached for his phone to call the police and then thought about having that on his record.

It would be his word against Howard's regarding who'd started the confrontation. Howard would bring up the suspicions of theft against Flint...

Leaving the vehicle running, he got out.

Stood face-to-face with the other man, his arms crossed.

"I'm here to help." Howard's gravelly voice didn't sound helpful.

"If she put you up to this, tell her that she can consider her conscience cleared. And while you're at it, tell her to stay off my property."

With a single bow of the head, Howard acknowledged the order. But didn't move. "You're a smart man, Flint."

He refused to let the compliment distract him.

"Too smart to risk losing your daughter without doing all you possibly could do to keep her."

*They knew.*

Glancing at the door of the day care, he realized he should've known. Michael had said he had to provide Diamond's day-care information. Tamara had recommended Mallory to him.

They were all in it together.

Like hanging with like.

Sticking together.

That was how things worked.

"She's my sister, not my daughter." It was all the fight he had in that second, while he figured out what Howard was after and then did something to circumvent whatever it was.

"She won't know the difference until after you're more father than brother to her."

Point to Howard Owens.

The admission was like a slug to his shoulder. Nothing more.

"Let me help you."

He stared at the older man. There'd been a real plea in his tone. He'd never taken Howard for an actor. Never knew he had that talent.

Stood to reason, though, considering his wealth and the business he was in, convincing people to part with their money.

Flint's business, too. His one real talent.

"Why?" he asked.

"Does it matter? You don't want to lose that baby, you need a job."

"I'll find a job."

"Not with almost a decade's experience, not with a book of business large enough to impress even the most jaded of judges, not one that's going to give you the security you've got at Owens."

"Until you fire me for fraud, you mean."

"We got our man," Howard said, giving him nothing more on that.

He wouldn't have expected anything different. Howard would be bound by a legal agreement not to discuss the matter.

"There'll be a next time."

"Probably not before your custody hearing." Howard didn't even blink.

"I don't accept pity."

"Not even for your little girl?"

He had him there, and Flint made a fast decision.

"Thank you, sir. I appreciate the offer. I'll move back into my office this morning. Would you like to send word to my clients that I'm back from sabbatical or should I do that?" The question was a real one, and issued with sarcasm, too. He wasn't dishing up a load of respect to the man.

"I'll do it. I have a few things I'd like to say to them on your behalf. And then you do what you damned well please. You're the best I have and I need you on board."

Now, that made sense to Flint.

He nodded, got in his car and drove off.

Later that week Flint got a call from Howard Owens. Sitting at his desk, he picked up.

"I misjudged you," the older man said.

"Yes."

"In the numbers business, the money business, we play percentages."

Flint more than Howard, and yet it was true.

"The percentages pointed at you," Howard noted.

"Years' worth of faithful and diligent service, coupled with high returns, don't rate well with you?"

"Most of the traders on staff have that."

Also true. "I'm your top earner."

"You were making plans to leave."

This conversation was going nowhere.

Or it had already arrived there.

He got Howard's point in making the call.

"Thanks for getting in touch," he said, his tone more amenable. He'd just received an explanation from Howard Owens. A collectible to be sure. Because of its rarity.

"I was wrong. I realize now that you were planning to do it right, Flint. I want you to know how much I appreciate that."

Damn. The man must've seen his bottom line drop significantly over the week of Flint's absence.

"Just glad to be back, sir," he said, determined to get busy and earn his future job security.

Which was all Howard had to offer.

He didn't kid himself about that.

A week before Christmas, just after Tamara had arrived at work Tuesday morning, Mallory called.

"He asked me not to say anything, and I haven't, but I think what you said about him is right, Tam. Flint doesn't ask anyone to help him and I'm really afraid he's going to lose Diamond."

"It's because he doesn't trust that anyone *will* help him," she said, having reached that conclusion sometime over the past week of thinking about him. About them. About herself, too. She took for granted that there'd always be people around her who would help her out.

Flint had never known a day in his life where he could take anything good for granted. Least of all the people around him.

"Tell me what's going on," she said. She'd called him a couple of times since he'd been back at Owens Investments, almost grateful to get his voice mail so that she could just say what she had to say.

She'd told him how sorry she was. She said she understood that the issues between them, including her aversion to motherhood, would always keep them apart, but that she wanted him to know she loved him and that if he ever needed anything, she hoped he'd call her.

She'd asked that he let her know about Diamond. Told him how deeply she believed the child belonged with him.

He'd called back the last time. When she'd answered, he'd simply told her to cease calling him and then hung up.

Very clearly she'd been warned.

He could keep her from contacting him, but he couldn't control her heart.

Love chose her. She most assuredly didn't choose it.

"The DNA must've come back positive," Mallory told her, "because Flint has to take the baby to court for a hearing this afternoon."

Tamara was just wrapping up her job with the box-making company she'd been working for since leaving Owens. She expected to be out of there for good by late afternoon.

"It's just a hearing, though, right? Nothing happens today, even if a decision's made?"

"From what I understand—and he's not too chatty with me since he knows I talked to you about him last week—it could go one of three ways. He could be given full custody, with the grandparents getting some kind of visitation rights. They could get joint custody. Or the grandparents could get full custody with him having visitation rights.

"I think he only told me that much because the outcome will affect Diamond's time here, as well as who can pick her up. He said he's going to request that in the event they get joint custody, the Reddings agree to continue bringing her here on a regular basis so her life has as much stability as possible."

Heart pounding, Tamara stood from the temporary desk she'd been clearing off. "You think there's really a chance they'd decide custody today?"

"He sure seems to think so because he said he'd let me know if she'd be here tomorrow. I guess he had an in-home study done over the past week, and I'm assuming the Reddings did, too. It's my understanding that they live somewhere in the area."

"So the case is being heard here in San Diego?" Tamara.

"Yes, I know that because I had to fill out a form, answering questions, and send it in to the court."

The hearing would be at the courthouse. She could find out the room when she got there. "Do you know what time the hearing is?"

"I know it's after lunch because he's picking her up at noon."

That was enough. "Gotta go," she said, thinking furiously. "Thanks, Mal."

"Just help him, Tamara, and then for God's sake, let yourself be happy."

She didn't really get that last part. But couldn't think about it, either. She was one hundred percent focused on devising a plan to change a course of life events and only had until noon.

*You're going to be someone.*
*You're special. The best part of me.*
*Don't you ever give up.*
*You're going to be someone.*

With the baby carrier on his arm, his tiny girl asleep and completely unaware of where they were, Flint walked into the courtroom just before two that afternoon.

He'd never met the Reddings, but knew instantly who they were when he saw the couple sitting at the table on the right, holding hands.

Her hair was brown, probably dyed based on the evenness of the color, her dress a cheery shade of rose.

Rose for Diamond Rose.

He was in full military dress.

Good move.

Flint didn't have a chance in hell in spite of his hand-tailored shirt and three-hundred-dollar shiny black shoes.

Much smaller than he'd expected, the room had only two benches for spectators behind the two tables facing the judge's bench. He'd been told the hearing was closed, but to expect a caseworker, probably Ms. Bailey, in addition to attorneys for both sides. Michael had also warned him that the Reddings could call witnesses on their behalf if they chose.

He'd been given the same opportunity, but had no one to call.

Certainly not Stella Wainright. He'd be back in court in two days for his hearing with her.

Merry Christmas.

He could feel the older couple staring in his direction as he pulled a chair next to him for the baby carrier and took his seat at the table. He didn't glance over.

It occurred to him that they probably wanted a glimpse of their granddaughter. All they had left of their only child.

He didn't blame them.

He just didn't like them. Or rather, didn't like that they existed.

Michael arrived and the hearing began shortly after. Flint had purposely timed his arrival so Diamond wouldn't be in court any longer than necessary. He'd tried to time her feeding so she'd sleep through the whole thing, too, but she hadn't been interested in lunch at one thirty. He hoped the little bit she got down would tide her over until he got her out of there.

Because he was going to get her out of there.

He had to believe that.

And he did, right up until he heard the voices of Grandma

and Grandpa Redding, heard their tears and the love they had for a child they'd never even met. Their own flesh and blood. The only grandchild they'd ever have.

Maybe Diamond would be better off with them, after all.

He had to get outside himself, his own sorry feelings, and do what was best for her.

Trouble was, he couldn't seem to get far enough outside himself to believe that she was better off without him.

Being the child of a convict... It was tough. Like Howard Owens had said, people went for percentages. And chances were, if you came from a life of crime, you'd be more apt to get involved in a life of crime.

People were always going to judge you accordingly.

Which tipped the scale even further toward a life of crime.

But that didn't mean you had to make that choice.

He *knew*.

And could teach her.

And while she was the Reddings' only grandchild, she was his only family, period.

He'd had his chance to speak. Had said some version of all that. He couldn't remember exactly what he'd said as he sat back down, but he could tell by the worried frown on Michael's face that he had to prepare himself for a best-case scenario of joint custody.

Which meant a life of upheaval for Diamond. She'd never have one place to call home. Or the same place. She'd never be able to come home day after day, week after week, to the same family. Or spend Christmas with the same people every year of her growing up, making memories they all shared.

He hadn't had it, either, not all the time. But he'd sometimes had it. Even when home had been a dingy trailer with a hole in the bathroom floor that looked down onto the dirt below, he'd preferred being with Alana Gold over the nicest of foster homes.

The Reddings had a couple of witnesses. A preacher. And someone else. Flint spaced it.

"If there are no further witnesses, I'm ready to issue my decision."

"Excuse me, Judge." Flint looked over as his attorney stood beside him. "I do have another witness to call—or rather a group of them. They weren't sure they were going to make it, but I just received a text that they're here in the courthouse. If I may ask the court to be patient for just another minute or two..."

The judge, a man of about fifty, not far from the Reddings' age, glanced over his glasses at the couple, at Flint and then at the baby carrier beside him. He seemed like a good guy. Flint didn't blame him for deciding, as he probably had, that the Reddings could give his baby sister so much more than a single man, son of a convict, could. In the obvious ways, at any rate.

"A child's future is at stake," the judge said after a long minute. "Of course I'll wait."

Agitated as hell, Flint scowled at Michael. "What's going on?" he whispered.

Michael leaned over. "You want to learn to trust that someone will actually help you, or just hand her over?"

He didn't like the man's tone. But sat straight, turning when he heard the door behind him open.

If Stella was pulling some prank, trying to play nice only to annihilate him...

Howard Owens walked in with a woman Flint had never met. The way her arm looped through his made him figure he was looking at Dr. Owens. Tamara's mother.

A fact that seemed more obvious when Tamara walked in right behind them.

In a pair of navy dress pants, and a navy-and-white fitted top, with her auburn hair falling around her shoulders, she looked stunning.

Just stunning.

He was stunned.

Because behind her, more people were filing in. Men, women, all in dress clothes. Rich men. Rich women. In rich clothes. A politician. The police commissioner. A college president. He knew, because he knew them all.

He'd talked to most of them that week, assuring them that their portfolios were solidly back in his hands.

"Your Honor, these people all know Flint Collins personally, have known him, and trusted him, for years. Most of them for more than a decade." Michael proceeded to introduce them, one by one, begging the judge's pardon for a few more minutes to allow each of them to relate just one piece of information about Flint's ability to provide Diamond Rose Collins with a secure and healthy home. The home her mother had chosen for her. Because she'd known her son.

Flint could hardly hear for the roaring in his ears. The tightness consuming him. He couldn't take it in. Couldn't comprehend it.

But before anything else could happen, before those around him could speak, his baby girl, maybe distressed by all the people gathering around them, started to cry. He shushed her quietly. Rocked her carrier. But the wails grew louder. He had a bottle, just in case. Was reaching for it, feeling heat rush up his body, when he noticed that someone was beside him. He caught a whiff of flowers. And then feminine fingers were expertly unlatching the carrier straps, Diamond was up, held in Tamara's arms, and the crying had stopped.

Tears in her eyes, Tamara faced the judge.

"I am in love with Flint Collins, Your Honor. These are my parents." She nodded to Dr. and Mr. Owens. "Flint felt he had to fight this on his own, but that's not what family's about. Yes, he had a challenging upbringing, which means he doesn't yet know how extended family works, and that's why we're here to show him. I've had the honor to be in this little girl's life since the day she came home to Flint, and I am fully prepared to be in her life until the day I die, just as any biological mother would."

Her words, a little hard to understand at times through her tears, were no less effective. Not where Flint was concerned.

Diamond lifted her head, throwing it back a bit, but Tamara's hand was right there, steadying her. She looked at Tamara and then laid her head down on Tamara's chest again, closing her eyes.

"If it pleases the court, I've got something to say," Howard said.

The judge shook his head. "I don't need to hear any more."

Just as quickly as Flint's hope had risen, his heart dropped. Until Tamara took his hand. When he looked at her she was grinning, for him only. Holding his gaze. Telling him something important.

He might not know a lot about family, but he wasn't a stupid man. He held on to her hand.

"After giving this matter consideration, I feel it's in the best interests of this particular child to honor her mother's legal wishes by giving sole custody to her brother, Flint Collins…"

The man's voice continued. Flint heard mention of the

Reddings working out visitation times with Flint. He heard some technicalities. And a comment about hoping to see them back in his court again for the young lady to officially adopt Diamond.

He heard it, but couldn't believe it. None of it.

"Court dismissed." A gavel sounded.

It made no sense to him.

He was going to wake up. Find out that he was still in bed, it was Thursday morning and he had to face getting up, knowing he might lose Diamond that day.

Except that Tamara's fingers were digging into his palm. People were gathering around him. Patting him on the shoulders. Dr. Owens came up to his side, opposite her daughter, put her arms around him and gave him a hug.

"Thank you," was all she said. Which made no sense to him, either.

He nodded, though. Because it seemed appropriate.

And as soon as he could, he turned to Tamara, put his arms around her and hugged gently, feeling how hard she was trembling. With an arm still around her, he took his baby girl in his other arm and knew he was never going to let go. Of either of them.

He'd done what he'd had to do.

He'd just become somebody he'd never known he could be.

## Chapter Twenty

The tree was lit, Diamond had been fed and was asleep in her swing, steaks were ready to grill, and Flint stood in the kitchen, opening a bottle of wine.

Christmas Eve, and he wasn't working.

He'd put on the black jeans, the red sweater. He had gifts wrapped and under the first tree he'd had since he'd left for college, and he still couldn't quite believe he was going to have a family Christmas celebration.

The Reddings had been over. Almost every day since their court appearance. They'd agreed that when Diamond got older, if she wanted to spend some weekends with them, she could, but for now, they were content to settle for babysitting. And visits.

When his attorney, Michael, had called Stella's attorney and, with Flint's permission, started dropping names of those on the support team who'd showed up for Flint in court, the Wainrights had dropped the charge against him. And then, when Flint's attorney had pressed, they'd agreed to sign a settlement to stay away from Flint and any member of his family and never to speak ill of him. Even after he'd refused to sign a similar one for them.

Tamara was on her way over after going to an early service with her parents. And he and Diamond had been invited to Christmas dinner at their place the next day.

Not so sure about that, having dinner at the boss's home, he figured he'd handle it like he did everything else. Standing up. Moving forward.

But for now, he had something more important to do.

As soon as Tamara got there.

He had a plan.

Because she was born to be someone, too.

Life had a funny way of working itself out, Tamara reminded herself as she climbed the steps to Flint's door on Christmas Eve night.

She'd sat through church, hearing about a blessed birth and feeling sorry for herself because she hadn't been blessed with the ability to give birth.

And then, ashamed, she stopped that train of thought. She was truly lucky. She'd been given a second chance with Flint, and she wasn't going to blow it.

Her issues weren't going away. She'd been unable to sleep for two nights after her day in court with Diamond Rose. But she was going to fight. Every moment of her life, if that was what it took. She was going to be in Flint's life. And that meant finding a way to let herself love Diamond Rose without falling apart.

She'd talked to Mallory right before church. Her friend was spending Christmas on a yacht in the harbor with some friends, and sounded like she was having a great time.

As good a time as it was possible to have during the

holidays when you didn't have family of your own. But Mallory wasn't giving up on life. Wasn't letting the past prevent her future.

Tamara needed to do the same.

Flint opened the door before she'd even knocked. He'd obviously been waiting for her and she loved that.

She took the glass of wine he held out to her, but leaned in to kiss him first. Long and slow and deep. He was much more delicious than wine.

They'd yet to consummate their relationship, but she hoped to rectify that situation this evening. The lacy red thong and barely-there bra she'd worn under a festively red-sequined sweater and black pants were there to help.

But when she began to make her move, he stepped back.

"I want to try something," he said, leading her into the living room. "Have a seat."

He seemed nervous, which was saying a lot. No matter what Flint was feeling on the inside, he didn't let weakness show very often.

So she sat. And wondered if he was about to ask her to marry him. It was a little early, considering they hadn't even slept together, and yet…it didn't feel early at all.

Except that she was a woman who might never be able to be a mother to his little girl. And who almost certainly wouldn't be able to have any more children with him.

"Drink your wine," he said, taking a sip of his as he told her about his day. About running out of tape in the middle of wrapping and having to go out and get more, his baby girl right by his side. She listened because he wanted her to. Sipped wine for the same reason.

But she really wanted to know what was going on.

When she'd all but finished her wine, he set down his glass. "I need you to try something with me. If it fails… well, then it does, but I feel strongly that we should try."

"Is this like one of those times when you take a risk on an investment because you're sure it's going to pay out, and then it makes you a load of money?"

"Kind of like that, yes. The feeling is the same. But I'm going to need you to trust me."

Though he prided himself on his knowledge, gleaned from studying everything he could about a particular topic, he'd been gifted with acute instincts. She'd learned that much about him very early on. Believed it was those instincts that had guided him so successfully through a life filled with hardship. Aided by what he'd learned, of course.

Her mind was babbling again. His nervousness was contagious.

She didn't know where he'd gone or what he was doing. Maybe seeing to the baby, although she hadn't heard a peep.

Then she heard his voice, speaking calmly. "Lie back and close your eyes."

An odd request, but he'd asked her to trust him. And she did. Implicitly. She lay back. Closed her eyes.

"Take me back to the day Ryan was born," he said, coming closer. She opened her eyes and he turned away. "No, please, Tamara, close your eyes and tell me about that day. Everything you can remember. Even if it's just about running out of tape."

She didn't like this. At all. But the tape? He'd focused on the mundane for a reason, so she did, too. Because she trusted him.

She was safe with him. Emotionally safe. And so she did as he asked, sharing that day with him in the little things, things that hadn't mattered to anyone else who'd talked to her since her son's death. She remembered that she'd had chocolate for breakfast—in the granola bar she'd eaten. That she'd shaved her legs. She'd had a day off work. Had gone in for a haircut and had wanted to leave the salon. To be home.

Her car had half a tank of gas.

The weather was warm, balmy. The sun shining. She'd thought about picking a cucumber from her garden to have with cheese and crackers for lunch. Wanted to remember to call her mom.

He asked her what she was wearing that day, his voice so soft she almost didn't hear him. So soft, he didn't break her spell. And she told him about the pregnancy pants. Not leggings, but real pregnancy pants with the panel. Her friends had teased her, but she'd wanted them because she was actually showing enough to need them.

The maternity top had been blue with little white, red and light blue flowers.

She talked and talked. Remembering so much. Relaxed from the wine. And the goodness of the feelings that had welled up in her that day. The hope.

But it didn't stop there. In the same soft voice, closer, right next to her on the couch, Flint asked her to talk about the first labor pain she'd felt. What she was doing. What she was thinking.

One second at a time, through the little things, the thoughts she could remember, she went through that horrific afternoon with him, including every moment she remembered in the hospital, talking about the sounds, the voices she heard, other people's conversations.

A conversation about babies who'd been born at her gestational time period surviving and eventually thriving.

She took him with her through the pain of the birth, the silence when she'd expected to hear a baby's cry. The look on the doctor's face. On Steve's face. She'd known. They hadn't had to tell her, she'd known. Her precious baby boy hadn't survived the birth. Tears streamed down her face as she felt the hysteria building inside her. Steve told the doctor to give her something and—

Just before the darkness came… "Stop." Flint's voice was still soft. The command was not to be denied. She lay there, eyes closed, and waited.

"Do you want to hold him, Tamara? Just once? To say goodbye?" His voice. She started to sob. To sit up. To lash out and—

Gentle hands against her face. "Keep your eyes closed, Tamara. Stay with me. Trust me. It's okay to cry, sweetie. Just tell me if you want to hold him."

She was back in that hospital room, right before the darkness.

"Yes," she said. "Yes, I want to hold my baby."

"Here." Flint's arm slid behind her back, supporting her weight as he lifted her, straightening her a little. Something touched her chest and she reached up automatically, cradling it.

The weight was slight. He was only four pounds.

"He's in a blanket, Tamara, wrapped up and warm. He looks so peaceful. Don't be afraid to hold him tight. You can't hurt him."

Of their own volition, her arms closed around that bundle. She didn't think to question, to wonder what it was. She just held on for all she was worth. Crushing it to her. Aware that it had more give when she squeezed than a human body would, but she was holding him. Eyes closed, lying there against Flint, she was holding her baby boy.

She cried. Hard. And Flint held her. She lay there until Diamond's cries broke the spell. And then, when Flint didn't move, she opened her eyes, told him she was okay and urged him to go care for the baby.

He didn't bring Diamond in to her. She'd thought he might, but knew he'd made the right choice.

She was still sitting there, holding what she now knew was a teddy bear, weighted and stuffed with a gel-like pillow pad.

Her trials weren't over. She was well aware of that, and Flint was, too. His gift to her hadn't been a cure, hadn't been meant as one. Flint was too much of a realist for that. And it was clear he'd done a lot of reading she hadn't known about. Studying her situation. Giving her the gift she needed most of all. He'd given her what no one else had even tried. A chance to hold her own baby boy.

Mostly, Flint had just sat with her in her pain. Taking some of the weight of it from her.

Flint grilled the steaks. He picked at his dinner just like Tamara did. And when she said something about maybe heading home, he asked her to spend the night.

Not to have sex. Just to lie in his arms and sleep.

Diamond was old enough to spend a night in her nursery. He'd keep the monitor beside him.

He'd had it all worked out and was still surprised when she agreed.

Leaving a T-shirt and boxer shorts on the end of his bed, with a cellophane-wrapped toothbrush—compliments of the dentist—on top, he told her he'd get the baby fed and down and would be back.

"Just get in whatever side you'd like," he said, growing hard as he pictured her in his bed, and yet, not achingly so. Some things were more important than sex. "The remote is on the stand there. Find whatever you'd like to watch."

By the time he got back, she was asleep.

Tamara woke with something warm against her back. She couldn't figure it out at first and then memory came crashing back.

Flint. He was spooning her. In his bed.

She had no idea what time it was, but felt like she'd been sleeping for days. Deeply. It was still dark outside.

Diamond Rose. Had he fed the baby?

Listening, she heard a little sigh and then even breathing coming through the monitor.

It was a good sound.

A very good sound.

There were other good things, too. Like the arm looped over her side, holding her close. The...ohhh...pressed up against her.

It was growing.

In his sleep, or had she woken him?

She wanted him awake.

Turning her head slowly, she kissed his chin. Or what she thought was his chin. He moved and caught her lips with his.

He must've said something because she was back in a trance again. Letting him take her away, to a different place this time.

A much happier place.

With an incredible ending.

But when they lay together, exhausted and complete, she didn't feel as though anything was over.

"Marry me," he whispered in her ear.

"I want to, Flint, so badly, but I can't do that to you or Diamond. That little girl deserves to have a mother who can hug her all the time and let her know how much she's loved. Kids need to be hugged."

"She needs *you*," he said. And when she shook her head, he asked, "You want me to tell you how I know?"

She nodded.

"When it comes to Diamond, you've got a mother's instinct. That's what makes mothers special. It's not something you buy. Or even learn. It's something you have that makes a kid feel okay even when things aren't okay. It's what my mother had."

"I don't have that." He was romanticizing now. So not like him.

"When you came into my office that day, I couldn't do it for her. I didn't know what she needed. You did and you didn't hesitate. She quieted immediately. That was no mistake, Tamara. Surely you've been around crying babies in the past few years, but you've never walked over to pick one up and quiet him or her."

Yeah, but…

"Anytime I talked about Diamond, you seemed to know instantly what she needed. What I needed to do."

Well, that had just been common sense.

"And in court, I was going to lose her…we were going to lose her. And you swooped in and saved us. Not just by being there, but when she started to cry…she needed a mother to seal the deal and you became one. You are one. She looked at you, laid her head down and closed her eyes."

"I—"

He put a finger to her lips. "I don't have all the answers yet," he told her. "I don't have any more at all right now. I might not ever have them. But I know that you're meant for us, Tamara, and we're meant for you. It's all up to you now."

He knew what he was getting into and wanted to take it on. Take *her* on. Maybe even needed to. He'd never even told her he loved her. She imagined that didn't come easily to a man like Flint. But he'd showed her. In a million different ways.

Mallory had told her to let herself be happy.

No one could do it for her.

"Yes."

"Yes, it's up to you now?"

"Yes, I'll marry you."

She was done with letting her past prevent her future.

They made love a second time and still didn't fall asleep afterward.

Maybe he was waiting for Diamond's next feeding. A couple of hours had passed. She had too much on her mind to let sleep take over.

"I want to try again," she said, feeling sick to her stomach even as she said the words. "Not right now. Not anytime soon, but I want to have your baby. Our baby."

"We have our baby, Tamara," he told her, sitting up and pulling her against him. "Biologically she has two other parents, but she's all ours. And if at some point, we're sure you're ready, then we'll face whatever happens together."

*Whatever happens.* Because you couldn't control life. You could only control what you did with what you were given.

Which was why Flint had grown out of an environment of crime into a remarkable man.

Diamond's whimpers came over the baby monitor. Slipping into a pair of shorts, Flint went in to change her.

"I'll get her bottle." Tamara, wearing an oversize T-shirt of Flint's, was already on her way to the kitchen. She was the bottle-getter when she was in the house.

But when she went to the door of the nursery to drop it off, she didn't let it go.

She wanted to hold the baby. To sit in the rocker and know she could be a mom.

She started to shake.

"Bring her in with us," she said. "Just while she eats. I'll sit up to make sure we don't fall asleep."

Without saying a word, Flint did as she asked, setting the baby down in the middle of the bed, half lying beside her and reaching for the bottle. Tamara still didn't give it to him. Kneeling on the mattress, keeping her distance, she leaned over. Diamond Rose looked at her—that little chin dimpled, lower lip jutting out—and started to cry. With the baby watching her, needing what she had, expecting Tamara to give it to her, there was no thought. From her distance, Tamara guided the nipple to that tiny birdlike mouth as though it was the most natural thing in the world.

Because it was.

For a mom.

\* \* \* \* \*

*Don't miss the next book in*
*The Daycare Chronicles, available March 2018*
*from Harlequin Special Edition!*

*And for more by Tara Taylor Quinn,*
*be sure to look for*

Fortune's Christmas Baby

*her first contribution to The Fortunes of Texas,*
*coming in December 2018.*

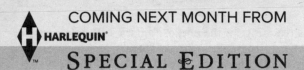

# Get 4 FREE REWARDS!

## We'll send you 2 FREE Books plus 2 FREE Mystery Gifts.

**Harlequin® Special Edition** books feature heroines finding the balance between their work life and personal life on the way to finding true love.

FREE
Value Over
$20

---

## SPECIAL EXCERPT FROM

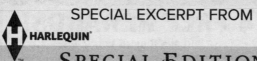

**HARLEQUIN**

# SPECIAL EDITION

*Arizona park ranger Vivian Hollister is not having a holiday fling with Sawyer Whitehorse—no matter how attracted she is to her irresistible new partner. So why is she starting to feel that Sawyer is the one to help carry on her family legacy? A man to have and to hold forever...*

*Read on for a sneak preview of*
**A Ranger for Christmas,**
*the next book in the Men of the West miniseries*
*by USA TODAY bestselling author Stella Bagwell.*

She rose from her seat of slab rock. "We'd probably better be going. We still have one more hiking trail to cover before we hit another set of campgrounds."

While she gathered up her partially eaten lunch, Sawyer left his seat and walked over to the edge of the bluff.

"This is an incredible view," he said. "From this distance, the saguaros look like green needles stuck in a sandpile."

She looked over to see the strong north wind was hitting him in the face and molding his uniform against his muscled body. The sight of his imposing figure etched against the blue sky and desert valley caused her breath to hang in her throat.

She walked over to where he stood, then took a cautious step closer to the ledge in order to peer down at the view directly below.

"I never get tired of it," she admitted. "There are a few Native American ruins not far from here. We'll hike by those before we finish our route."

A hard gust of wind suddenly whipped across the ledge and caused Vivian to sway on her feet. Sawyer swiftly caught her by the arm and pulled her back to his side.

"Careful," he warned. "I wouldn't want you to topple over the edge."

With his hand on her arm and his sturdy body shielding her from the wind, she felt very warm and protected. And for one reckless moment, she wondered how it would feel to slip her arms around his lean waist, to rise up on the tips of her toes and press her mouth to his. Would his lips taste as good as she imagined?

Shaken by the direction of her runaway thoughts, she tried to make light of the moment. "That would be awful," she agreed. "Mort would have to find you another partner."

"Yeah, and she might not be as cute as you."

With a little laugh of disbelief, she stepped away from his side. "Cute? I haven't been called that since I was in high school. I'm beginning to think you're nineteen instead of twenty-nine."

He pulled a playful frown at her. "You prefer your men to be old and somber?"

"I prefer them to keep their minds on their jobs," she said staunchly. "And you are not *my* man."

His laugh was more like a sexy promise.

"Not yet."

#1 *New York Times* bestselling author

# LINDA LAEL MILLER

### presents:

The next great holiday read from
Harlequin Special Edition author Stella Bagwell!
A touching story about finding love, family and a
happily-ever-after in the most unexpected place.

*No romance on the job—*

Until she meets her new
partner!

Arizona park ranger
Vivian Hollister is not
having a holiday fling with
Sawyer Whitehorse—no
matter how attracted she
is to her irresistible new
partner. Not only is a
workplace romance taboo,
but she has a daughter to
raise. So why is she starting
to feel that the Apache ranger is the one to help carry on
her family legacy? A man to have and to hold forever…

**Available November 20,
wherever books are sold.**